ADVENTURES WITH ATHENS

A NOBLE GLOBAL QUEST

KEM ARFARAS

❄Special Dedication

Thank you, God for giving me the confidence to believe in myself and for turning my book into a reality. And to my son Athens for being the inspiration to all my stories, my mom for believing and investing in me. To my husband for his time and faithfulness of 35 years. To my precious four grandchildren who are the animal characters in the story, along with two special girls - Annabelle and Savannah Greenman for their added inspiration and love in my life.

adventureswithathens1@gmail.com

www.adventureswithathens.com

Soon to come are more Adventures with Athens for all ages.

Illustrator ~ Sierra Carter

Author ~ Kem Arfaras

© 2020

Fifth Edition

PROLOGUE

Come along for an epic quest that begins in Athens, Greece and travel the world through secret portals to all seven continents in seven days.

Do you love adventure, mysteries and discovering new things?

Meet Athens and Abigail, who are best friends that have the same dream and are sent on a special quest to fulfill their destiny. Seek out hidden treasures and ancient relics in hopes of discovering six sacred pieces of armor that were crafted in the heavenly realms before their time. Find out how Athens and Abigail make new friends and overcome their fears along the way.

Is your name written in the Lamb's Book of life?

Uncover evil forces that lurk in the shadows of the unforeseen places of the earth. Boldly stand before the gods and kings of past and present in search of Truth. Who is the true King of Kings? It's believed that The Kingdom of Heaven is where the streets are perfected with gold. Does such a kingdom really exist? Will they fulfill their quest in time for the royal banquet and be crowned heirs to the King's throne? Or will they fall into a black hole for all eternity?

Learn about natural phenomena around the world as you dive into this wonderful book and discover things you never knew existed!

Table of Contents

CHAPTER 1

THE KING OF KINGS

BELT OF TRUTH

Athens, Greece

ONE BRIGHT AND EARLY MORNING, in the heart of Greece, lived a brave, adventurous young man named Athens. Sound asleep, deep in his cozy bed, Athens had the most amazing dream. He had fallen asleep next to his glowing moon lamp while reading one of his favorite books. On his dresser lay a lion and a lamb figurine, a long shofar horn, a unique rock collection, and some Holy oils from Israel. Athens' bedroom looked like a scene right out of a movie.

On the wall above his desk was a framed polished award that read; *Athens Arfaras - A True Blue Panther-Awarded Exceptional Student of the Year.* His collection of books filled with adventure, fantasy, and mystery were neatly placed along the wall on a large wooden bookshelf. It was no wonder he had such imaginative *dreams ... But this was in no way an ordinary dream.*

Athens had been chosen to carry out a noble, global quest by order of the Most High King.

A booming noise was heard throughout heaven when a burst of shooting stars fell from the sky and came crashing down to Earth, followed by a seven-headed ten-horned great red dragon wearing seven crowns upon his head. He was attempting to devour Athens and his best friend, Abigail. As Athens armed himself, twelve legions of angels came bolting out of the clouds with thunder and lightning. The angels' enormous wings spanned across the sky and circled high above their heads, preparing for battle.

Suddenly, the voice of God shook the atmosphere and called out to Athens, giving him a glimpse of what was yet to come. ***"Do not be afraid, for I am with you."***

Athens tossed and turned in his sleep and became entangled in his sheets. Without warning, a loud trumpet blasted. Athens opened his eyes, awoken by the great sound. Two swords and a shield hung on his wall that he had forged with his own hands. Beneath that was a large map of the earth. He sat up and peered closely at it. His eyebrows creased together when the compass on the bottom of the map started spinning out of control. Suddenly, it stopped spinning and pointed right at him. He blinked twice and rubbed his eyes then bolted out of bed and ran downstairs to the kitchen, where his mother stood by the stove, preparing breakfast.

"Mom, you're never going to believe it, I can hardly believe it, but I just had the most incredible dream!"

Athens' mother turned around and looked at him with curiosity. "What did you dream about?"

"I dreamed I was in the presence of God, and He chose me to carry out a great quest to find the Truth and fulfill my destiny!"

A hint of amusement sparked in her eyes as she raised one eyebrow. "Really, and what truth would that be?"

"The truth about the kings of old, the truth about which King reigns supreme, the truth about who I am and why I'm here." He boldly answered as he stood there with the palms of his hands pressed against his temples.

"Wow, that's some dream!" said Mrs. Arfaras

"It was incredible. In my dream, there were six sacred pieces of armor supernaturally crafted in the heavenly realm. The armor was made to protect, defend, and stand against dark and evil forces. Each armor piece is unique and has a different purpose, but together as one, they can defeat the enemy and conquer the evil in the world."

He stopped and paused for a moment, taking a deep breath, then sat at the table and fiddled with his fork. "My mission is to collect all six armor pieces, learn their purposes, and conquer my fear. My life depends on it. Only then will I come face to face with King Elohim on the seventh and final day. Guess what else?"

Three knocks rapped on the front door. Mrs. Arfaras walked into the foyer while Athens poked his head around the corner. Who would be here so early in the morning? The door cracked open. Athens could see it was Abigail, his best friend. She stood in the doorway with the light shining on her long dark silky hair and rosy cheeks. "Abigail, what are you doing here?"

"I came to tell you the good news. I had a dream and, you were in it. We traveled to a faraway place called the Promised Land, a land flowing with milk and honey… a place where the greatest treasures in all the world exist. There's a mighty King that lives there. This King is not just any ordinary King, but one who has supernatural gifts and extraordinary powers and authority. He can raise the dead and change the entire world as we know it! His name is King Elohim. The King of kings, Lord of lords, and the Host of hosts."

"Wait, what?" Athens rubbed his temples. "That's incredible! You were in my dream too." A wide smile spread across his face as he looked into Abigail's big brown eyes.

Abigail laughed. "Once all the pieces are discovered and delivered to the King's mansion, we will become heirs to His throne and receive a great inheritance. Imagine being free to do whatever we want whenever we want for the rest of our lives."

"Who would've ever thought right here in our hometown, right under our very noses, such a quest would arise?"

Athens moved his eyebrows up and down, then looked out of the corner of his eye and caught a glimpse of what was outside the kitchen window. Just beyond the olive trees and herb garden, the Acropolis sat on the peak of the hill, overlooking the great city of Athens.

"Yes, indeed, that's where we'll begin. No better place to start than right in our own backyard," Athens turned toward his mother and opened his arms as he pointed out the window.

The patio vines seemed to magically come alive as the leaves danced and twirled around the columns. Mrs. Arfaras stepped outside onto the patio to feel the breeze.

"I believe you are destined to do great things. Interestingly enough, when you were a baby, I would catch you cooing and giggling while grasping at the air with your tiny little fingers and toes as if you were talking with an angel. And on occasion when you were a little older, I'd hear you talking to God in your sleep when I'd go in to check on you late at night."

Mrs. Arfaras grinned. "Back in the day, many kings and queens of ancient Greece lived very rich lives. They commanded their kingdoms and built temples to worship their gods. They have all risen and fallen over time. The only thing left of them are their giant stone statues and storehouse treasures. Rumor has it, that their spirits still live and walk the earth to this very day." Athens and Abigail went over to the french doors and stepped out onto the patio.

"I can't even imagine what it must have been like living back then. Oh man, I almost forgot, in my dream, the King had a book called *The Lamb's Book of Life*. Only those whose names are written in it will be allowed to enter His kingdom."

"I can hardly wait. This is going to be the best adventure ever. But why do I have butterflies in my stomach?" Abigail whispered while biting her fingernails.

"Do you know how you got your name, Athens?" his mom asked. Athens shook his head.

"Well, then let me tell you," she said.

"Names are very important," Abigail interrupted. "My name in Hebrew means my father's joy, and Kyriacos, my last name, in Greek means of the Lord."

"Yes, you have a beautiful name," Mrs. Arfaras said, as she turned her attention back toward Athens. "I've never told anyone this before, but I prayed and fasted for three days, asking God to bless us with another beautiful baby. After patiently waiting, God revealed the answer. Then one day, while I was standing on our hotel's rooftop, overlooking and admiring the view with your brother, sister, and father. We could see the entire city and ancient ruins of Greece. It made me think about you and what name we should give you. Your sister came up with the idea of naming you after the great city of Athens. As we thought about the idea, it became clear that this would be a great name for you, it means wisdom and courage. Your middle name Seth means a promise renewed. So, you are quite unique." she said, as she ruffled his hair.

"When we visited local shops, before you were born, the shop workers gave me little trinkets because they wanted to bless the new baby to come. That was you! Now, here you are, preparing for this noble, global quest."

Mrs. Arfaras walked inside the house and went over to look at a baby picture of Athens hanging on the wall. "We were going to surprise you for your birthday and give you an extraordinary gift. But since it's so close to your birthday, I'd like to give it to you today. I think you'll need it for your journey."

"What is it?" Athens asked.

"I can't tell you. It's a surprise. You'll have to wait until your father gets home from work to make sure he approves of this quest first, but I promise you, you're going to love it. Now, tell me more about your dream."

"If we make it through the golden gate and meet the King in person, all of our dreams will come true as promised. His mansions are made of gold with precious stones and jewels. Even the streets are made of pure gold. We will be appointed heirs to His Mighty Kingdom for all eternity," Athens paced around the room with his hands on his hips.

"My favorite part is the grand celebration and royal banquet that will last for seven amazing years. We'll be blessed beyond measure if we survive the journey and make it through all seven continents in time." Abigail twirled around the room.

"God hasn't revealed everything to me, but He's given me some clues to get started." Athens said as he tapped his finger on the side of his temple. "Note to self; I need write down the names of all the places that I'm traveling to, so I won't forget. I'll need a map too." He ran to his room and grabbed an Atlas, then returned to the kitchen and began turning the pages.

"Where will you go first?" Asked his mother.

"Our journey begins on the hilltop of the Acropolis." He pointed out the window to the city of Athens. Then paused, realizing he didn't want her to worry about the deceptive dragon, demons, and dangerous creatures of the night, so he decided to leave that part out. "Next is Egypt, then to Australia, after that is Rio de Janeiro, Brazil; then we go to Deception Island in Antarctica.

On the sixth day we should be in Yosemite National Park, California and on the seventh day we will arrive in Israel where we will meet our destiny. Every country is riddled with mysteries and hidden treasures waiting to be discovered. Israel is set apart as the greatest of them all. If I find the Truth and finish the quest in time, I will fulfill my destiny. The downside is that I only have one day to find each armor piece in each of the cities and deliver them to King Elohim's mansion by the end of the final hour on the seventh day. Ugh! I don't know if I can do it. What if I fail?" Athens' shoulders drooped.

"You're not going to fail. You'll have me by your side. After all, that's what friends are for," Abigail leaned in closer and gave him a nudge.

"First, you must have faith, believe in yourself, and trust that God will guide you. Start thinking and acting as if you've already accomplished it, like a true prince!"

"Come over here, please," Mrs. Arfaras extended her hands and led them in a little prayer.

"Heavenly Father, thank you for allowing us to come before You with our requests. You are the Alpha and Omega, the Beginning and the End. You are an amazing father and friend. Please protect my son and Abigail." She paused for a moment and lifted her head. "They're Yours before they're mine. Their hearts are faithful, ready, and willing to serve. Please give them all they need to complete the task, including faith, hope, and courage. We ask that You soften Mr. Arfaras' heart and strengthen his faith. Please remove any worry, doubt, or fear that he's struggling with. Thank You for all You've done, for all You are doing, and for all that is yet to come. Amen!"

Opening their eyes, the three nodded their heads to agree with one another. "I need to know that God is with you and that His angels are protecting you so that I won't worry about you two. Let's hope God softens your father's heart. You know how he feels about traveling, not to mention the fact that this will be a total life-changer, you've never traveled alone before."

"Yes, it's true. However, I still want to get ready, I need to be prepared." Athens quickly ran upstairs while Abigail went home to talk with her grandmother.

While brushing his teeth, Athens gazed into the mirror at his olive complexion and rich dark wavy hair, trying to imagine how he would look standing next to the King, wearing a royal robe, a golden ring, and a crown of jewels upon his head. He grinned as he touched his face. He could hardly wait to tell his father, even though he was afraid his father would not allow him to go. "God, please let my dad approve of this journey." Athens believed that God would somehow make it happen if it was truly His will. With everything going on, Athens completely forgot to eat breakfast. Just thinking about the banquet feast, seeing and tasting all that great food for seven incredible years made his mouth water. He looked at the clock on the wall and continued counting down the hour until his father arrived home from the sponge docks.

When he finally heard the front door close, he knew it was time, so he dashed into the living room to greet his dad. Mr. Arfaras had a peaceful glow and a gentleness about his face that Athens had never seen before. He knew something unusual must have happened but didn't know what it was. He stared into his father's light green eyes. "Dad, I have something to tell you."

"Yes, I have something to tell you too, but you go first," his father replied.

"God came to me in my dream. He's called me on a global quest to seek out the Truth and fulfill my destiny."

"Yes, God does want you to fulfill your destiny. I know this to be true because an angel of the Lord appeared to me and spoke earlier today." Mr. Arfaras took a deep breath then let out a sigh. Athens knew at that moment; this was an act of God. His dad would have never allowed him to travel across continents alone. But, this was no ordinary quest. It was a divine appointment ordered by the Most High King.

"God's quest for your life is great. But if you change your mind about wanting to go, I'll understand. It can be a little scary and crazy out there, even for a brave and daring young man, such as yourself. However, there could be great consequences to pay if you choose not to go because He's already called you to it. Just remember son, our family name means everything to us. Our honor is at stake."

Athens' dad squeezed his shoulder, then walked over and sat down on the couch in the living room. Athens went over and sat next to him.

"I understand, Dad. I'm honored that He has chosen me for this quest. I'll do my best not to let you or Him down." Athens patted his dad on the back and smiled.

Mrs. Arfaras ran upstairs, remembering to get Athens' gift. She held it tightly behind her back as she headed back downstairs. With a warm heart and gentle smile, she spoke, "now, close your eyes and no peeking." She carefully placed the gift into his hands. The wrapped gift felt round and smooth as he gripped it with his warm fingers. What could it possibly be? His imagination was bursting with ideas.

"Okay, open your eyes!"

Slowly opening his eyes, tears of joy and sorrow streamed down his mother's cheeks. His heart was heavy. "Why are you crying?"

"I can't believe this day has come. It seemed like yesterday when you were a little boy, and now you're a young man. I'm happy for you but sad for me because I'm going to miss you. I'm honored to call you my son."

Athens smiled, then looked away, trying hard not to get choked up. He couldn't help but turn his eyes toward his unopened gift. "Go ahead and open it," Mr. Arfaras said.

Peeling away the wrapping paper was like opening a window into heaven. An amazing onyx globe filled his hands. He rolled it around and around, viewing it from every angle. The brilliant gemstones were stunning. Each glimmering precious stone had been carefully hand-selected from around the world and cut precisely into the shapes of all seven continents. Each one was inlaid with exotic gold trim.

He stared deep into the globe, and watched it glow as glorious beams of light shot out of its inner core.

"Wow! How is this even possible? This is unbelievable."

The colored stones sparkled in every direction, filling the entire room. The light was so intense and bright. It created supernatural streaks of rainbows that illuminated their faces. A vision of heaven appeared above their heads like a golden aura of glory. They stood in awe, gazing upon this marvelous light of hope.

"Now, you definitely have something to look forward to," his father suggested as he stared in awe at its beauty while his mother clasped her hands together and held them near her heart. "Your destiny awaits you. God's clearly moving in our lives." She said.

After seeing a glimpse of what was yet to come, Athens was eager to get started on his journey. He gently wrapped his globe in a soft white cloth for safekeeping and put it in his backpack. Three knocks wrapped on the door, and this time Athens knew it would be Abigail. His heart jumped with excitement as he ran to the door.

Upon arrival they stood at the top of the Acropolis in the courtyard garden. Athens' mother anointed their heads with her sacred oils of frankincense and myrrh while Athens' father led them in a powerful prayer asking God Almighty to bless them, protect them, and give them the peace and wisdom they'd need for their journey. Mr. and Mrs. Arfaras hugged their necks then waved goodbye.

"Athens!" His mother called out as she ran over to him. "Remember to keep your promise to God hidden. You'll know what to do at the right time." She gave him one last hug. A tear trickled down her cheek. Mr. Arfaras swallowed hard, fighting back the tears, not knowing when or if they would ever see them again as they watched Athens and Abigail fade into the background.

Abigail gave Athens a curious look, not knowing what they had talked about but she was hoping he would tell her at some point, but for now, the search was on. They looked for the place where he had envisioned his dream. He felt the urge to walk toward a gigantic rock formation, not knowing that a beautiful angelic being was waiting for him.

Her eyes sparkled and her face was glowing as bright as a radiant star. She moved towards Athens and spoke. "Hello, I've been waiting for you."

"Wait, what?" Athens' eyes were brightly bulging as he raised his eyebrows. He had no idea who she was because God had not revealed her to him in his dream. He had a million questions racing through his mind but only asked one. "Who are you?" He was surprised and mesmerized by her beauty at the same time. Her golden blonde hair and bright blue eyes kept him staring.

"Do you want to know the truth, or shall I make something up for you?"

"The truth, of course! Telling the truth is always the best thing to do, even if it's not what you want to do."

Abigail moved closer to Athens. "What do you mean by the truth?" she asked.

"The Truth, you know, believing in something based on facts or evidence, even if it doesn't benefit you. Trusting reliable information is what we all need to make up our minds about what we believe." The angelic being gestured around them. "Look at all these stone statues. It's easy to make idols out of the gods and people. Sometimes you can take the wrong things too seriously.

You have to be careful not to let your own desires and selfishness get in the way of God's plan."

Athens picked up a pebble off the ground and threw it. Then looked around at the circle of the gods and goddesses carved out of stone. One of the male figures held a pitchfork and stood next to a three-headed dog. They almost looked real. There was a female goddess statue holding a spear in one hand and a shield in the other. She looked troubled.

Abigail was peering off to one side. "Oh, that truth, I totally get it. We often want what we want without asking ourselves why we want it, which can lead to trouble if we don't search for the truth first. Sometimes, we're blinded from the real truth and say things that aren't true because we want to believe in something else if the truth doesn't make us feel good."

"Do you ever ask yourself why you want something? Do you ever tell yourself no? Does any of this make sense to you?" Asked the angelic being.

"Yes, it makes perfect sense. If we want the Truth, sometimes we have to dig for it until we find it," Abigail replied while shuffling her feet in the dirt.

"Staying focused on the quest ahead, seeking God's desires instead of our own will lead us to the truth," Athens said. "Now, will you please tell us who you are?"

"I'm your guide. My name is Eliza, which means God is my oath. I've been sent here by the Most High God to assist you."

"You mean God Almighty sent you?" Abigail asked.

"Yes, The God of your dream. He's not just any god. He's the greatest God and King of all the ages. He's the creator of the Universe, the Heavens, and the Earth."

Athens walked over to the statue of Zeus. His eyes seemed to look right through him, while Abigail wandered around viewing other statues.

"You will soon discover that the God of the universe has many names. He created every good thing there is and created you for such a time as this. He wants you to complete this quest by seeking the Truth with all your heart, mind, and soul. Remember to be true in all you think, say, and do. You must turn away from evil when confronted by it. Only then will your destiny be fulfilled." Eliza pointed to the statues. "Some gods, like Apollo, and Hades, were mighty in their day, but their powers were limited. Take the goddess Athena, the goddess of wisdom, or Aphrodite, the goddess of beauty and love. They were worshiped in these very temples. Their powers didn't go beyond their region, but please don't misunderstand me; they were all compelling in their day. They sat on their thrones and had great authority over the dominion of the Earth."

Without warning, a bolt of lightning fell from the sky and struck the statue between Athens and Eliza. One of the god's heads cracked and turned toward them as if it were going to speak, but Athens wasn't about to hang around to find out what it had to say. He bolted out of there as fast as he could and came upon a statue of another god.

The title of it read *The Unknown God*. The face of this God was superior to the others. Its eyes were piercing,

its chin was raised high, it had a strong masculine jawline. Athens was fascinated at the sight of it.

Eliza appeared beside him like a beaming light.

"The gods were seekers and lovers of themselves," she whispered. "They were always looking for other gods to join them but never recognized the *Unknown God* as the One True God who *"Was" and "Is" and "Is yet to come."* This *Unknown God is* different. He's pure and good. Not selfish like the others. He doesn't hurt people or desire worldly gain." She pushed her hair behind her shoulder and continued. "The demigods got what they wanted when they wanted it because no one was there to challenge them. They did as they pleased, wishing to be as the One True God. They used their powers to influence the world, destroying anything and anyone that got in their way. They wanted to control everything, especially people. They rebelled against the One True God, which was their greatest downfall. Their world came crumbling down, putting an end to their empires."

Eliza ran her human-like hand along the smooth marble stone statue. "Everyone must choose their own path. You may not always immediately get the rewards you want for doing what's right, and that's okay. God will reward you in His perfect time, even if you have to wait a while. It'll be well worth it."

Athen listened to her speak as he followed her along the path. "Everyone has a choice to make," he added.

"A choice to do good or evil." Eliza said looking down at her hands, "look at the choices in front of you and pretend like you're holding them in your hands. Take the truth and put it in your right hand, and put the lies in your left hand. If you have trouble deciding which one to choose, put your hands together and pray."

Athens peered down at his hands and folded them together. "Great point. I need to remember to do that from now on, not that I ever plan on lying, but it's a great idea for any tough decisions that I have to make."

"Did you know that you can ask God to help you make the right choice?" Eliza spread her arms wide open. "You alone hold the key." Ask yourself the hard questions, then ask God to show you the truth and give you the strength to do what is right."

<u>His power starts in your mind and moves to your heart and then to your hands.</u>

Athens' eyebrows rose. He was impressed by Eliza's ability to shed light on the truth. She led him over to a large solid rock near the cliff to stand on. She pointed to the rock. "This rock is your foundation. It's like your cornerstone. You must be standing on it when you depart from each of the secret portals. It allows you access to each of the continents. This is where your faith steps in. Without a solid foundation, you can't stand against the evil in the world, nor will you be able to move between continents. Only if you speak the words of truth will you be granted the power to access the portals."

She leaned in close to whisper in his ear. "Say these words only while standing on the rock, only when you are ready to move to the next continent, and you will arrive speaking the language and wearing the clothes of the country you are entering. All of this is to help you blend in with the culture around you, so you won't appear to be an outsider."

"Whoa!" Athens eyes grew big as he shook his head and stared down at the rock.

"Are you ready?" she asked.

Athens wiped his sweaty palms on his shirt and nodded as Eliza spoke the words. "Guide me in Your Truth and teach me Your ways, oh Lord, for You are my God, my Savior, my hope is in You all day long. Repeat the words three times to help you remember what to say at first because, without the exact words, there is no way to enter or exit any of the secret portals."

Athens began speaking the powerful words when he realized Abigail was no longer beside him. Where is she? He mumbled under his breath. "She has a habit of wandering off. I'm sorry, she gets easily distracted."

They looked toward the hilly, grassy area by the brick watering well. From a distance, Athens could see her behind a cluster of butterflies fluttering around the well. Abigail had her arms outstretched and laughed when one landed on her nose. Athens walked toward her and watched as she touched the unusual flowers around the well. Some looked like little miniature monks kneeling and praying, and others looked like white doves sprouting from their stems.

He continued watching as she climbed onto the ledge. Athens was guessing she wanted a closer look. She closed her eyes and leaned in to smell the sweet fragrance of the nectar that filled the air. When she opened her eyes, a beautiful mammoth butterfly landed on her shoulder.

Athens kept walking toward her as she eyed the intricate detail of the butterfly. Then, she turned her head to gaze into the sparkling pool of water in the well. *Was Abigail admiring herself, he wondered?* Her reflection was like a sparkling ray of sunshine mirrored in the water. Her long dark silky hair, rosy cheeks, and beautiful big bright eyes were dazzling.

Suddenly, she leaned in a little too far and fell into the well. Athens gasped as he witnessed a giant splash of water spill out of the well. He quickly ran over to help her. He peered down into the deep hole as she spiraled out of control. He stretched out his arms to grab her, but he couldn't reach her. It was too late. She extended her arms and legs to slow herself down, but the water pulled her downward, with no way to stop. She was sinking deeper into the abyss. This wasn't any ordinary well. It was dug so deep that it seemed endless. She screamed for help, words bubbled out of her mouth, although no one could hear her. Athens was about to lose sight of her, he knew he had to save her. *But how?*

He looked around and noticed a bucket and a rope with something shiny and silver attached to it. There was no time to unwind it. He quickly picked it up and felt a jolt of electricity surge through his body. He tossed it into the well while keeping a firm grip on one end.

Could this be the Belt of Truth? Strangely, he began to see the words *Truth, Hope, Faith, and Love* swirling around in the water, encircling her body. He watched as the words floated to the surface. *Were those Abigail's words, or were they wishes of other people?*

The magical belt wrapped itself perfectly around Abigail's waist, not too tight, not too loose. Athens took a stance as he tugged and pulled with all of his might. Slowly, pulling her up to the surface, she finally reached the top. The weight of the pull knocked him backward. He fell, hitting his bottom on the ground. Abigail was breathless, choking on the water before spitting it up, then she gasped for air. Dripping wet from head to toe, she stood there with her big brown eyes, and droopy hair as tears streamed down her cheeks.

"I almost drowned." She sobbed. "I panicked until I saw the long, silver shiny belt that appeared in front of me. I was so vain to admire myself the way that I did. I was looking at my reflection in the water when I leaned in a little to far and fell in. I'm so sorry. Will you please forgive me?"

"I'm proud of you for telling the truth. I'm not judging you. We all have our faults. But you know, true beauty comes from within. I'm just glad you're okay. This could have ended very badly if the belt hadn't been visible in time." Athens wrapped his arm around her and comforted her.

"Thank God for the Belt of Truth. It saved my life."

Eliza walked closer. "You need to be more careful. The temptations you'll face are your own struggles that you need to learn to deal with. I'm so glad Athens responded when he did.

"You must think about what you're doing and why you're doing it. Don't let your heart be troubled. Never compare yourself to others. Everyone is unique and wonderfully made. I don't want to frighten you, but danger will be

lurking around every corner, so I want you to be strong and mindful of your actions." Eliza smiled then put her hands on her hips. "Let's go over and finish preparing for your departure."

They followed her back to the rock but couldn't see anything until she motioned her hands in front of their eyes, allowing them to see the rock. "Ahh, a step of faith," Abigail said as she waited to step onto the stone.

"When you're standing on the rock, you'll be standing on a firm foundation that you can trust because it's solid. Have you ever heard the term solid as a rock or rock-solid?" Eliza asked.

Athens nodded his head as he prepared his stance. "You know, it's something you can trust. It's not going to let you down. God is the same way. He allows us to walk through life's challenges, but He always walks through the hard times with us. Even when we're not paying any attention to Him, He sees and knows everything. Although we can't see Him, we can feel His presence when He's near." Athens put his hands out to feel the wind.

"Let's go over the words again to make sure you're ready," Eliza said.

Athens rubbed his hands together. He could hardly believe what was about to happen. Eliza gestured for him to stand on the rock before she spoke the words.

"Guide me in Your Truth and teach me Your ways, oh Lord, for You are my God, my Savior, my hope is in You all day long." Eliza pointed to Athens. "Now, you say it."

Athens opened his mouth to speak the words when Abigail quickly opened her mouth, moving her lips to mimic him. He looked at her and raised his eyebrows.

"Well, I'm preparing myself just in case you happen to forget the words," she said.

"Now spin around, then you'll disappear into thin air and reappear into the next continent. It all happens in the blink of an eye. Nothing to it, really." Eliza took a step back. "Remember where you're at by focusing on one thing that's right in front of you to help you find your way back to the hidden rock, look for a landmark of some sort. You must return to the exact location in order to move ahead. It's your only hope."

Athens pulled out the 3D onyx globe that his parents had given him. "We can use my globe to confirm our steps," he uttered with confidence.

"Your globe is quite remarkable," Eliza stated.

"I received it as an early birthday gift. It will give us the vision we need for our journey. We can see where we've been and where we're going. It has the power to show us glimpses of heaven too."

"It truly is the light of glory, it will definitely keep us motivated for the prize ahead," Abigail said.

Eliza reached out to touch the globe and put her finger on the continent of Africa. "Remember, when you get to Egypt, you'll search for the Breastplate of Righteousness in the Valley of the Kings. You only have seven days to complete the quest, which gives you one day in each continent. You must learn the meaning of each armor piece once you find them. It's of great importance for you to know how and when to use them. Each armor piece is unique and performs in different ways. You'll face many battles that you could have never imagined. As you collect each piece and put them on, your powers will grow, and so will your faith." Athens held the globe close to his chest as he leaned into the light of hope. Abigail stretched out her hands to touch it and was amazed. Eliza looked at Athens intently. "Guard and protect your heart and mind. Don't let anything come between the two of you."

Athens and Abigail stood firmly on the rock and held hands before Athens spoke the blessed words. A gust of wind blew in and spun them around, then carried them away.

Fun Facts:

- The description of Athens' room and how he got his name is true. He received the True Blue Panther award in 8th grade at Pine View Middle school for being an exceptional student of the year. (Being thoughtful, courageous, excellent is his work and helpful to those around him).

- Genesis 1:1-31, 2:1 & 6:1-6 speaks of creation and of the demigods.

- Peter 3:13-15 tells us that God will reward us for doing what is right.

- Athens loves forging with fire and making knives, blades, and axes. He's also learning how to make bows and arrows from trees that he has cut down.

- He has two shofar horns and many sacred oils from Israel. The horns are blown during feasts and festivals in Israel every year and the oils are used for anointing God's chosen ones.

- Athens has an Onyx globe trimmed in gold from Greece that was purchased before he was born and given to him for one of his birthdays.

- The exotic flowers around the well are real and look like monks before they blossom into doves. Page 27.

- In Athens' backyard on his Papaya tree are caterpillars with white crosses on their foreheads. See if you can find the small caterpillar in one of the pictures.

- Athens' middle name is Seth. It means a promise renewed. He is the third born of Adam, just like Seth in the Bible is the third born of Adam and Eve. Genesis 2:5-25. Jesus was born through the lineage of Seth. Matthew 1:1.

- The Lamb's Book of Life, also known as; The Book of Life! In Daniel 12:1, Luke 10:20, Philippians 4:3, 20:15. Revelation 3:5, Revelation 20:15.

- *__God's Trinity: His power starts in your mind: The Father and moves to your heart: The Holy Spirit then to your hands: Jesus Pg. 23__*

- Read more about the Belt Of Truth on page 164.

CHAPTER 2

WHO'S THE RIGHTEOUS ONE ?

BREASTPLATE OF RIGHTEOUSNESS

The Valley of The Kings, Egypt

" **W**hoa, that was so awesome! My fingers are still tingling, and my body feels as light as a feather. I think we just traveled through a time warp at the speed of light!" Athens exclaimed.

"I feel a little dizzy from the transport, but I can't wait to do it again, it's definitely awesome." Abigail replied.

Nighttime came upon them as they stood on the rock's edge near the Nile River, wearing their charming Egyptian clothing.

A moment later, Eliza showed up like a ray of light to warn them of the dangers ahead. She explained. "The Valley of the Kings is a dangerous place after nightfall."

"It's where robbers and strange creatures go lurking about, seeking to devour their prey."

Athens didn't seem to be too worried about the dangers ahead. *But shouldn't he be worried?* He seemed more curious about the Valley of the Kings and the ancient tombs of Egypt. He wondered which kings from the past were buried in the royal tombs. He could only imagine what they were thinking when they built such secretive tombs for themselves. He envisioned them eating and drinking and living merry lives.

Athens bent down and picked up a half-broken piece of clay tile from the floor bearing the marks of a sphinx. "What do you know about the kings of old?" he asked.

Eliza straightened her stance and folded her hands together. "Well," she said with confidence. "Around 500 BC, King Tut, King Ramses, and many other Pharaohs lived rich, lavish lives with the hope of someday escaping the clutches of death. They created burial tombs made of sandstone and were laid to rest deep within the valley walls. They built secret chambers for ceremonial purposes to preserve their royal dead bodies and made great preparations to celebrate in the afterlife once they returned from the dead. This was their grand scheme. All their jewelry, gold, and royal dishes laid next to them."

Eliza continued. "Unfortunately, their plans never worked. They didn't realize that no amount of silver, gold, or gods could ever bring them back to life to live their rich extravagant lifestyles they once knew. Treasure hunters and tomb raiders stole almost everything. Thieves kept most of the treasures for themselves. Everything else was destroyed or placed in museums."

Athens and Abigail stood listening with their arms crossed as Eliza spoke. "It's believed, the kings and pharaohs of old never recognized the One True King, the One who could have set them free and given them the greatest gift ever known—the gift of Eternal Life. The King of kings loves all people of every color, rich and poor, young and old alike."

Eliza pointed to the east. "There's only one place marked on the face of the earth where such a mighty King was born. A place where we will soon go. This King's tomb was no ordinary tomb. In fact, it was made deep in the heart of the earth for a rich man. Yet, this humble King borrowed it for three days and three nights before rising up from the grave. His death, burial, and resurrection became known throughout all the land. This One True King gave His own life as a ransom to save billions of other's lives, including yours and mine. Only a righteous King would do such a thing for His people."

Abigail unfolded her arms, "You mean everyone lives forever?"

"Yes! That's exactly what I mean. The One True King wants to save every lost soul on the planet, and He wants to help every single person come to know and accept the truth by finding Him." Eliza's eyes turned crystal clear as she looked at both of them. "His intentions are good, not evil. He wants you to have love, peace, and harmony in your heart. It can't be bought, sold, or taken away from you, no matter what others will say or do."

Athens smiled, then looked up into the heavens and noticed a spectacular vision of starlights in the night sky.

"I can see Leo the Lion in the constellation."

Abigail pointed to the Big Dipper and the Little Dipper too. Eliza directed them to the north, showing them the Star of Bethlehem. She told them it had not been seen for over 2,000 years. It was the brightest star in the sky and was back for all the world to see. It was yet another heavenly sign of the One True King.

A grand and fierce lion with a beautiful golden mane appeared on the horizon with his pack of pride. He raised his head in the air as if he could smell their human scent from afar. The king of the jungle took a step forward to catch a glimpse of them, sizing them up for a possible meal. Athens looked off into the distance and spotted the herd of lions sitting on top of the hillside behind their king. These majestic animals were a reminder of who was in charge of the animal kingdom. The lion kept the title — King of the Jungle, although the lioness does most of the hunting. Athens shuddered. He certainly did not want to be their next meal.

Looking ahead, he saw the crossroads leading down separate paths. Right when he was trying to decide which way to go, something blew across the ground and stopped at his feet. He bent down and picked it up. He had never seen anything like it before.

"This is a Resurrection plant, also known as the Rose of Jericho," Eliza explained. It can last for years without water. It tumbles around on the ground like a tumbleweed in search of water until it finds some, then it stops to drink it up and blossoms into a flowering plant wherever it happens to be. It never needs to be planted in the ground."

"Magnificent," Abigail replied.

Athens touched the plant briefly with his hands and tilted his head to examine it closer. Then he shifted his weight on one foot and set it back down. He turned around and noticed a sign with many arrows pointing in different directions. The first one read *Lincoln the Lion's Den*. It was facing a long narrow path leading to the hillside. Another sign pointed down a broad and crooked path that read *Lucifer the Dragon's Lair*. It had a big X painted over it. The third sign pointed down a skinny bumpy path that read *Jaxon the Jaguar's Cove*.

Eliza advised Athens to choose wisely. "One path will lead you in the right direction while the other paths will lead you astray."

None of the options were what he wanted, but if he had to choose one, he'd choose the narrow path toward the lion's den. No way would he choose the broad way leading to the dragon's lair.

"It's time to choose," she urged.

Just then, a handsome young man with dark hair, a round face and cute dimples appeared on the same path that they were on. He picked up the Resurrection plant and put it in his bag. "This plant is exactly what I need," he said as they watched him. "This plant will bring me good luck and can make me rich. I bet I can make a fortune selling them in the marketplace. I just need to learn how to grow them first."

"Come on, we've got to go," Athens said as he fixed his eyes on Abigail.

"Excuse me, but where are you going?" asked the young man.

"We are on a grand mission searching for six sacred armor pieces. Right now, we're looking for the breastplate.

Our final destination is in Israel. Anyway, who are you?"

"Addison's my name. I'm on my way to Israel too. Do you mind if I come with you?"

Athens looked into his eyes, hoping he wasn't just another distraction. He shrugged his shoulders then spoke. "Sure, you can join us if you're up for an adventure. This trip is not for the fainthearted, and you'll have to leave the plant here. Where we're going, you won't need to worry about money."

He started to laugh. He thought Athens was joking until he realized no one else was laughing. He kindly returned the plant to the ground and the three of them walked toward the lion's den. They passed through golden fields of wheat and lavender before reaching the Valley of the Kings. The wonderful scent of lavender went directly into their noses.

Without warning, a fierce male lion, likely Lincoln the lion, rustled the field in front of them. His tawny coat and golden mane were visible above the wheat field while his pride was sneaking up behind them for a surprise attack. It was likely Lincoln who let out a tremendous roar as he stood in the field, gazing hungrily at Athens and his friends. Athens shook with fear but stood on solid ground as he held up his hands and shouted, "Stop!"

The other lions slowly moved in for the kill and formed a perfect circle around them. They were surrounded. Athens remained brave. If he couldn't get the lion to listen, they'd all be lunch meat.

"I said STOP in the name of the One True King!" Athens yelled in a booming voice. Lincoln was about to leap into the air to pounce on him when an angel of the Lord appeared and stopped him. They were quite shocked to see what Lincoln did next. Instead of eating Athens and his friends, he stretched out his large paws, then bowed before them. The Spirit of God led Lincoln to provide Athens and his friend's protection against the wild things of the night.

"Forgive me, master Athens. I didn't realize who you were." Lincoln the lion said.

Stunned that the animal could speak. Athens hesitated then answered. "No problem, thanks for not eating us."

Lincoln no longer had the desire to eat them. Instead, he led them to a secret entrance into the Lion's den, where they gazed upon a giant monument carved out of the mountainside. Hidden by dense vines was the opening of the den shaped like a gigantic lion's head with a wide-opened mouth. It had sharp pointy teeth formed from the edges of the stonewall. The lion's paws and claws were enormous. Those, too, were carved from solid rock. On the wall above their heads, they found an inscription that read: *Only the righteous one with a pure heart should dare enter into this dwelling, lest you die.* No one else wanted to go in, except for Athens and Abigail.

With God's help all things are made possible. Abigail said.

"You wait here," Athens insisted, but Abigail lifted her chin and said no. "We both had the dream, and I'm coming with you."

Athens smiled and took out his onyx globe through the darkness. Its inner light beamed bright, stretching deep into the cave and magically made a passageway that opened up into an inner chamber filled with magnificent armor. There were so many breastplates and armor pieces that filled the room, Athens couldn't possibly know which one to choose. He stopped to think, then turned to the right and turned to the left before kneeling on one knee. He wondered which breastplate would represent his King. He closed his eyes, trying to imagine which ones were used in battle and which one may have been worn by the High Priests of the Royal Priesthood. He wondered what it was like living back in those days and who would have worn the Breastplate of Righteousness? He thought about his options, then placed his hands together and began to pray, asking God for wisdom. He emptied his mind of any thoughts he had about the breastplate and waited for God to reveal it to him. When nothing immediately came to mind, he slowly got up, trying his best not to get impatient. He walked around the room while waiting for an answer.

Moments later, he looked over to see what Abigail was doing and realized she was gone. He wanted to go and find her but needed to keep searching for the right breastplate. He touched row after row of armor and noticed they were made of different types of metal, silver, and gold. Some of the pieces had emblems and relics indicating royalty and majesty, while others had images of animals with wings and half-human, half-beast faces with swords and crosses on them. None of those stood out until one particular breastplate caught his eye from a distance. It had the characteristics of something sacred and holy that only one with a pure heart would wear. It was adorned with twelve of the rarest gemstones ever known to man. Each stone had brilliant glowing colors. The armor was made of gold, purple, blue, and scarlet fine twilled linen. The shoulder straps were attached by golden braided chains with gold ring bands that bound two sizable black onyx stones on the tops of each shoulder. The breastplate had twelve unique stones with twelve names of the tribes of Israel above them engraved in gold.

With a tug on his heart and a hungry mind, he moved towards the reflective light coming from the breastplate. Instantly, it shimmered and shined when he touched it. He placed his hands on his chest as his heart raced at the sight of it. At last, he had chosen wisely. Without another thought, he picked it up and boldly placed it over his head to cover his torso. It was a perfect fit. But it wasn't what he had expected. He stared in amazement. He thought it would be solid metal, like what the Roman soldiers wore into battle, but it wasn't. Then it hit him. An explosion of confidence came over him as he stood dressed in the Armor of Righteousness.

He followed a trail, hoping it would lead him to Abigail, but instead, he came across an opening in the valley where many dry bones were scattered across the ground. He wondered whose dry bones they were when he saw an ancient textbook lying in the rubble. He knelt down, then brushed it off, and was about to open the book when two black jaguars with razor-sharp teeth and claws

focused on him. One raced toward him, then lunged into the air, and pounced on him, pinning him down to the ground. Two stones burst forth out of the vest from the force of the hit and landed next to him. His heart was thumping so loud he could hear it. He stretched out his arm in agony as far as he could reach, trying to grab the two precious stones. These were no ordinary stones, and he wasn't about to let the jaguar have them. They could only be used by God's anointed ones. And these were no ordinary jaguars. Athens saw a sharp intelligence in their eyes. Clearly, they were keepers of the armor, more specifically, the breastplate. It would be their job to stop anyone from taking it out of the valley. Perhaps this was Jaxon the jaguar staring deeply into his eyes. "Any last words before we devour you?" Jaxon asked.

Another speaking animal? Athens was stunned when the jaguar spoke and asked the question.

***

Abigail was fascinated by the great tombs deep inside the mountain. She searched for Cleopatra's tomb and knelt down beside a tombstone, then wiped away the cobwebs before reading it. Each word spoken out loud caused a stirring from within the sarcophagi where the mummies slumbered. As she read the list of names, loud groans and moans filled the air. Lids on the coffins creaked open and withered faces covered in bandages peered out. She had no idea she was summoning the mummies up from their graves. She had awoken them from their sleep only to find out they were still dead. Abigail trembled, her mouth dropped open. Her voice screeched thick with fear as it echoed throughout the cave. "Athens?"

Athens shouted in the jaguar's face. "Wait! I am the righteous one of God chosen to claim the armor. I must take it to King Elohim. It's one of six pieces I've been searching for, and I have to have it." The two stones began to glow and shine in Athens' face as he held them in his hand. A booming voice echoed from above. *"Do not harm him. Let him go!"*

"Thank God!" Athens whispered. The extraordinary jaguars were about to let him go when a third jaguar showed up unexpectedly and whispered in Jaxon's ear. "No, don't let him go. We can eat him for a midnight snack."

At that moment, Jaxon looked at the unusual jaguar very differently as if wondering where he came from. Jaxon told him to get behind him and not to interfere, but the hair on the back of the jaguar's neck stood on end as he opened his mouth and raised his sharp teeth, then growled. He turned against them and attacked. Jaxon lunged into the air, clamping down on the scruff of the jaguar's neck, and slung him into a stonewall, and swore to protect Athens as long as he remained in the valley. "Thank you for saving my life." The jaguar slowly lowered his head and winked. Astonished at what just happened, Athens returned his focus to the ancient book. He blew the dust off and quickly opened it.

The book's pages whimsically flipped back and forth until Athens put his hand in the middle of it to stop the flow. He was curious about the text and read the lines from the book out loud. *"Oh, son of man, hear my words."* Just then, a strong gust of wind blew in as

Athens read the book. The words magically flew off the pages and floated into thin air as they came alive.

He who has ears let him hear. "Can these dry bones live? Oh Lord God, only you know the answer! Prophesy to these bones and say to them, O' you dry bones, hear the word of the Lord! Behold, I will cause breath and spirit to enter you, and you shall live. I will bring forth muscles and flesh upon you and cover you with skin, and you shall return to your own land in Israel and live so you can testify that I am the living God, a sovereign ruler who calls for Truth and Righteousness."

Athens paused and took a deep breath. A loud thundering noise shook the earth's surface, and all the scattered dry bones began rattling and moving all at once. Human skeletons formed together and stood on their feet. Then organs, blood, and tissue covered their bones. New skin was shaped and stretched out over their muscles. Eyeballs were miraculously formed inside their sockets. The bones were now a host of men. There was no life in them until Athens spoke, then the breath of God flowed through them. Thoughts rushed through Athens' mind as he stood shocked by the whole thing before fleeing for his life. He raced toward the den to find Abigail and ran so fast around the corner he collided with an ancient mummy and stumbled backward. His big green eyes were bulging with fear.

This mummy wasn't in a crypt but stood upright, its bandages unraveling from the force of their collision. A piece of cloth had gotten caught on the corner of Athens' breastplate and wouldn't come loose. The mummy was acting frantic. It was moving its arms and legs wildly until it became completely unraveled.

But it wasn't a mummy at all. It was Abigail. She'd somehow gotten completely tangled up in the linen cloth, causing her to look like a mummy. Except they knew she wasn't one of them. Athens was relieved to find her and not some thousand-year-old mummified person coming after him. "Abigail, what are you doing?"

"I've been busy running from the mummies that I accidentally awoke from their sleep. They're coming after us! Let's go."

"How is that possible?" Athens asked.

"No time to explain," Abigail gasped. The mummies were coming from every direction. They ran for their lives as the mummies chased them back toward the valley of the dry bones. Standing at attention were the army of strong men waiting for Athens to hurdle past them. They charged full speed ahead to defend the righteous one of God. Athens and Abigail raced over to the rocks without looking back to escape the fighting. They returned to their secret place near the Nile River, hoping to find Addison and Eliza waiting for them, but no one was there. Athens knew there was no time to wait. They needed to complete their quest with or without Addison. They guessed Eliza would show up when she was needed.

Athens and Abigail stepped onto the rock and spoke the words. "Guide me in Your Truth and teach me Your ways, oh Lord, for You are my God, my Savior, my hope is in You all day long." In the blink of an eye, a gust of wind whirled around them and swooped them up into midair, causing them to instantly disappear.

Fun Facts:

- ·෫· The Breastplate of Righteousness truly exists and was worn by the High Priests of Israel. Exod. 25:15.

- ·෫· The Northern Star is the Star of Bethlehem, and has reappeared after 2,000 years since Jesus' birth.

- ·෫· The Resurrection plant, aka the Rose of Jericho blossoms, where ever it's at without being planted.

- ·෫· The story of Athens and the dry bones in the valley was created from Ezekiel 37 in the Bible.

- ·෫· The Valley of the Kings in Egypt is a touristy place.

- ·෫· <u>Look on page 166 to learn about the Breastplate.</u>

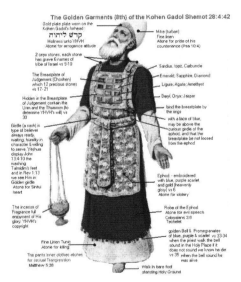

CHAPTER 3

A LEAP OF FAITH

SHOES OF PEACE

Canberra, Australia

Stepping off the rock into the heat of Australia's desert, Athens and Abigail became curious when they noticed a strange and distant wind blowing in from the south. Dark clouds blanketed the sky when a giant cluster of dust twisted and turned, forming a peak in the atmosphere creating a tornado. Two red eyes mysteriously formed right out of the center of it. Abigail scrunched her nose and squinted her eyes. "What is that?" she asked.

Could this giant dusty tornado be a dust devil? Athens looked at Abigail and asked, "Is that thing headed this way?" Debris was flying everywhere. In no way, shape, or form was this an ordinary dust storm.

The moment Athens spoke, the dust devil spiraled in their direction. The monstrous dust devil weaved back and forth after them as if it had a mind of its own. It grew stronger, and gained more speed with every step they took. Abigail's breathing became heavier as fear clouded her mind. There was only one thing to do - Run!

Athens felt the wind on his back as his spirit stirred. He pushed Abigail to move faster. They zigzagged across the dusty ground, kicking up the dirt beneath their feet, leaving a cloud of dust behind them. Seconds later, out of nowhere, came heavier winds from the west, stronger than anyone could have predicted. Huge winds spiraled in from every direction creating a massive whirlwind.

"That's not something you see every day," Athens yelled.

"Yeah, that's no ordinary whirlwind," Abigail replied.

Thick, dark clouds parted as the sky opened up. The fierceness of the wind whipped around in circles making a vast funnel coming down from heaven. Flashes of lightning shot out of the sky and created brilliant sparks and golden embers that made their way to the ground and caught some tumbleweed on fire. The tumbleweed rolled directly into the center of the whirlwind and made a blazing red fiery tornado. Abigail feared there wasn't enough time to escape either the fiery tornado or the dust devil. Athens glanced over at her and noticed her eyeballs bulging out of her head like a chameleon. "We're in big trouble." She said.

The fiery tornado could destroy them both and everything around them. Just then, a large troop of kangaroos came scurrying by to escape the tornado's fiery flames. One of the babies jumped out of his mother's pouch. "Oh no! Come on, Abigail, let's go get him." She didn't respond. Athens turned his head but didn't see her. She must have gone into the herd of kangaroos. Athens dashed after the little kangaroo to return him to his mother, but the little kangaroo was too fast. He couldn't keep up with him, so Athens shouted, "Hey, little joey, stop!"

Out of harm's way. The little kangaroo responded to Athens' voice and stopped in his tracks. Standing right in front of a small village, the kangaroo turned around to ask, "How did you know my name?"

Athens also stopped in his tracks. Wait, what. He thought to himself. *Did that baby kangaroo just speak?* When the animal repeated the question, Athens knew God gave him the ability to understand all the animals he encountered so far. "Well, I have a friend named Joey, and he's the fastest runner I know. You reminded me of him. Where are you running off to?" Athens asked.

"I'm not sure. I just got scared and ran away."

"Would you mind helping me find my friend?"
Athens asked.

"Sure," replied Little Joey.

"I have no idea which way she went, but I need to find her. I'm on a global quest, a grand mission, traveling around the world in search of sacred armor pieces. Right now, I'm searching for the Gospel Shoes of Peace."

Some of the local villagers were curious about Athens and Little Joey and came out of their beehive homes made of clay to see what was going on. They could hear

Athens talking but needed to get closer to listen to what he was saying.

"Either one of the tornados could kill us all and destroy the village. We have to get to safety!" Athens shouted.

"I've never seen anything like this before," Little Joey replied.

Athens said a quick prayer to his God. Afterward, things seemed a bit calmer and they both felt a little safer inside the village, hidden away from the dust devil.

"Who's your God, anyway?" asked Little Joey. All eyes and ears were listening.

"He's the God of the universe who created the heavens and the earth. He is the Alpha and Omega, the Beginning and the End. He guides and protects me and is here to help whenever I call on His name. You can call on Him too, and He will hear you. Actually, anyone can call on Him. He loves everyone and cares about what happens to us. He created us so that we can have a close relationship with Him."

"I can't see Him," said Little Joey as he looked around.

"True, but sometimes we can feel His presence, like the wind. I had a dream, and now I'm living it. God has gone to prepare a place in His Kingdom where there are many mansions. Even the streets are made of gold and shine as bright as the sun." Athens said.

"I get it now." Little Joey leaped into the air, and so did Athens, both laughing.

"In His Kingdom no-one will ever get sick or die. The things in this world are temporary, but the things we inherit from the Kingdom of God will last forever. He gives us the ability to accomplish great things when we trust in Him." Athens showed Little Joey the belt and the breastplate, he was stunned at the sight of it and wanted to touch it. But he was afraid to ask.

"You see, it's here in the desert somewhere that I have to find the Gospel Shoes of Peace before I can go to the next continent. I have to deliver all six pieces to King Elohim in four days to receive my inheritance."

In the distance, Athens noticed a distinct ancient tower of burnt ruins barely standing. It appeared as though smoke was coming out of it.

A woman from the village with sun-soaked skin and silver-lined hair spoke to him. She explained, "Long ago, people of every tribe and nation only spoke one language thousands of years ago. They tried building a tower to reach into heaven. But God didn't want them to because they were wicked people, so He caused them to speak in different languages, the people could no longer understand each other and they became confused and couldn't finish building their infamous tower. Soon, the town was empty, and the people moved away to rebuild their lives somewhere else. Only a few of us were left behind to carry out the traditions of our ancestors."

Athens had gotten sidetracked and before they knew it a massive burning tornado appeared out of nowhere. They had no time to run away. They had waited too long to escape. *Oh, but wait!* A magnified voice came from the fierce, fiery tornado and spoke.

54

"Athens, Do not be afraid. It is I, the Lord, your God, who is with you and will not harm you. Now step into the Holy flames and receive the Gospel Shoes of Peace."

Athens took a deep breath. God had kept him safe so far. He prevented the lion from eating him and the jaguars from attacking him. He had to listen and Trust that God would keep him safe. Athens swallowed hard, then obeyed the voice of God and stretched out his hands to touch the flames as he stepped into the fire. The glowing flames covered him from head to toe as he stood in the presence of God Almighty. Completely quenched by God's Holy Spirit, Athens was baptized by fire. Instantly, the Gospel Shoes of Peace were firmly fitted on his feet. With his eyes closed, he began praising God. His words magically became unrecognizable as he spoke in an ancient tongue, unknown to him. *But, how was this possible?* The villagers stared at him because they knew exactly what he was saying. When he opened his eyes, the flames of fire were still burning brightly in them. Not one hair on his head was harmed, nor did his clothes burn or smell like smoke. The peace of God was with them all. Athens looked down at his feet in awe. "Hallelujah," he shouted as a tingling sensation ran up and down his spine. He whispered, "I can't believe it. I'm wearing the Gospel Shoes of Peace, praise God!"

Without warning, the dangerous dirt devil came up from behind them, causing debris to fly all around them. Suddenly, the flames from the fiery tornado burst out from the center. Flaming orange arrows shot toward the dirt devil, disappearing directly into the dark, dusty center core. The twisting of the dirt devil slowed as if it were fatally wounded. But the Fiery Tornado didn't let up. It continued shooting fire into the churning center.

Finally, one of the glowing arrows set off a chain reaction. The dirt devil exploded in a mass of confusion, spraying sparks and dirt debris everywhere. It was totally destroyed. There was nothing left but a large dusty cloud of smoke and heaps of ashes. Little Joey's jaw dropped open. "Praise God!" He leaped with laughter.

Now they can tell others what they have seen and heard with their own eyes. The Fiery Tornado turned away from the village and vanished into thin air.

"Your God's powers are awesome!" One of the children from the village shouted.

"We are forever thankful, and we'll always remember this day." One of the women said.

"Glory to God, He really exists," someone else shouted.

Little Joey and the villagers witnessed their very first miracle. They thought the fire was going to kill them, but instead, it saved them.

Now that Athens has the Gospel Shoes of Peace he needed to get going and share the *good news* with others. "I'm on my way to meet King Elohim," he declared.

Little Joey jumped up and down. "Who's King Elohim?"

"King Elohim was the King in my dream. He's called me to complete this quest, and if I can accomplish it, I will become an heir to His Kingdom. I've learned the True meaning of His name — One True God. He gives the gift of Eternal Life to anyone who chooses to believe in Him."

"I believe, I believe!" Little Joey exclaimed. "Even though I can't see Him, I can feel His presence like the wind."

"God has given me a new spirit and a new heart, and it looks like you have one too. Let's find Abigail and your mom. I don't know which way Abigail went, so let's pray and ask God to help us." Athens bowed his head and prayed. "Lord of lords, King of kings, creator of all things, please help us find Abigail and Little Joey's mom. Most of all, thank you for protecting us from harm and for giving me the Gospel Shoes of Peace."

Athens continued praising God as he walked through the billows of smoke with Little Joey unharmed. Athens could see a troop of kangaroos on the other side of the village. As he walked closer, he wondered where Abigail was. Then, he saw her head pop up from behind the herd. He sighed in relief.

"I'm glad you're alright, Abigail. I was wondering where you were." Athens said as he hugged her.

Little Joey's mom hopped over and embraced her son, and kissed his head. "Thank you for returning my son. I was looking everywhere for him. How can I ever repay you?" she asked.

"No worries, ma'am. Although, I am a little hungry. Do you know where we can find something to eat?" Athens asked.

Out of the clouds, manna came pouring down from heaven like an unexpected rainfall. Everyone, including the villagers, looked up in disbelief. They held out their hands to catch the manna as they witnessed another miracle. They were so grateful for the abundance of bread that they began shouting and cheering, thanking God for all He had given them.

Abigail turned her eyes toward Athens' feet and noticed he was wearing the Gospel Shoes of Peace.

"Woohoo! Hallelujah!" she leaped into the air and spun around like a graceful ballerina. "Now we can go to Rio de Janeiro, Brazil, to find the Shield of Faith."

Athens turned his face toward Little Joey. "I'm sorry buddy, we have to go now. We're running out of time, but we hope to see you again sometime."

***

Athens and Abigail were on their way back to the hidden rock when Athens started thinking about the Great Barrier Reef. He was hopelessly curious and couldn't help but wonder what it would be like to swim in the great ocean for even just a moment. It was his lifelong dream. The sea's depths, the glistening blue waves, the coral reef and the cool ocean breeze, with the warm, soft sand running through his toes were all he could think about.

"Abigail, let's go for a swim. Right here, right now. My dream is about to come true. Let's do it." he said.

"I'm sorry Athens, I really don't want to go swimming right now. I think I'll sit this one out." she replied.

Athens without hesitating rushed over to the ocean, took off his armor pieces, placed them inside his backpack, and laid it on the sand, then stripped down to his shorts and dove into the deep blue sea.

Abigail quickly realized sitting was not something she wanted to do, so she decided to go exploring. She giggled as she walked along the sandy beach, when she spotted a super flock of birds wrestling along the ocean bank and decided to run through them for fun.

The birds squawked and squealed as she glided right through the middle of them. Hundreds of birds were everywhere. Some flew high, some flew low, and some barely moved at all. She was having a blast until she felt something hot touch her toe. *Ouch!* She reached down and sifted through the sand to see what it was. She picked up a shiny silver cross attached to a leather rope. It had an inscription that read, *God loves you*! She had a sweet grin on her face admiring her new treasure. Walking further along, she found herself at the entrance to a garden sanctuary. A sign was posted in bold letters that read, **Do not eat the forbidden fruit from the tree of life inside the garden.**

Curiosity itched her mind as she slipped into the garden. Just beyond the fruit trees, she found a beautiful painted forest of eucalyptus trees that looked as if an artist had painted their way through the forest by splattering brightly colored paint all over them.

She shuffled her fingers along the branches and touched the leaves as she smelled the lovely blossoms that floated into her nostrils. Peering into the trees further, she couldn't resist picking an incredibly plump and juicy apple, even though the sign said not to.

She turned around with the fruit in her hand. Just as she was about to take a bite, she felt something tug on the back of her hair. A warm, furry sloth reached out and wrapped one paw around her neck while holding onto the tree with the other paw. The creature stared at her as if admiring her, then dropped to one side, holding on tight. Abigail gasped, then smiled. "Whoa. What are you doing?" Intrigued by the cute sloth, yet stunned at the tug of her hair, she rubbed her tender head and took a closer look, face to face.

"Sorry, I didn't mean to scare you." The sloth slid down into her arms. "I should've introduced myself first." "I'm Savannah." Abigail was taken by surprise at the sound of a speaking sloth. She noticed the sloth had been previously injured by the looks of an old scar, probably by a poacher.

"Hi, I'm Abigail. How on earth did you get here?"

"I was brought here by a friend of the forest. Poachers were trying to capture me when I got caught in their net, but somehow I managed to escape. Now I live here in the garden."

"You're so cute. I'd love to take you with me, but I'm afraid you'd be in danger if I removed you from here." She hugged the sloth. "I have to go now. It was nice meeting you." The sloth just smiled and handed her another large apple before climbing up to a nearby branch. Abigail smiled, then turned and walked away.

"Now to remember which direction I came from." She paused and looked down at her feet. Footsteps approached her from behind.

"Glad I found you," Athens whispered.

Abigail jumped in surprise. Her hand flew to her heart. "You startled me." She exclaimed.

"I'm sorry," he chuckled. "I had the most incredible swim with a great humpback whale. It was the most graceful and gigantic creature I've ever seen."

"That sounds amazing. I'm glad you enjoyed yourself."

"Really?" He looked down at her hands and saw the two pieces of delicious fruit. "Where did you get the fruit?"

"It came from one of the trees in the garden forest. A cute sloth gave it to me."

"Didn't you see the sign at the entrance?" Athens asked.

"Yes, but I think it'll be okay. Something so delicious can't possibly be bad for you." she replied.

His eyebrows furrowed together. She gave him an apple, and the two of them ate a bit of the fruit at the same time. Almost immediately, their legs wobbled, their vision became blurred, their world around them went dark as they slumped down to the surface of the ground.

***

Eliza showed up like a twinkling light at the desert's edge near the hidden rock and waited for them. She noticed an inspiring male peacock spider moving on top of the rock, trying to capture the attention of a lovely female spider. He danced in the wind. After a while, one of them glanced his way and advanced toward him. All it took was one look for her to fall in love. The two spiders mingled and danced, then spun their way off the rocks-edge.

By this time, Eliza felt something was wrong in her spirit, so she searched for Athens and Abigail and found them lying asleep outside the garden gate. They must have fallen under a spell. She swiftly gathered some water and poured it over them. They immediately opened their eyes and gasped for air. It was near dawn on the next day. "Hurry up, you two! There isn't much time."

She helped them to their feet. "You won't get a second chance to meet the King," Eliza said, rushing them along.

"I see you didn't obey the sign that warned you not to eat the forbidden fruit. I hope it's not too late for you."

"Oh, about that, I'm sorry. I didn't have my armor on. I think it would've helped protect me," Athens held up his backpack that still contained the armor pieces.

"Yes, it would have." Eliza said as she hurried them over to the rock.

Athens spoke the powerful words. Then the pair quickly spun around and disappeared in a heartbeat.

Fun Facts:

- Fiery tornados and dust devils really exist in different parts of the world, especially in Australia.

- The Gospel Shoes of Peace are what believers wear on their feet to share the Good News about Jesus.

- Male Peacock spiders are very cool and really dance to find a mate. They are the size of a grain of rice!

- People around the world live in Beehive homes.

- The tower of Babel is in the book of Genesis 11:1-9.

- Rainbow Eucalyptus trees are native to the Philippines but grow in other places worldwide.

- Manna rained down from heaven during the Israelites 40 years in the wilderness. After entering the Promised Land it stopped once they ate the food from the land.

- See page 168 to learn more about the Gospel Shoes.

CHAPTER 4
CONQUERING YOUR FEAR

SHIELD OF FAITH

RIO DE JANEIRO, BRAZIL

Arriving in South America, wearing fun summer clothing Athens and Abigail were ready to start searching for the shield. Their view of the lush green terrain and unique tropical high mountain peaks were beautiful.

Eliza twirled in like a sparkling light. "Did I mention that you'll see one of the seven wonders of the world? It'll be life-changing for both of you. The whole world marvels at the magnificent sight of the *Christ The Redeemer* Monument. But before you begin your search, I have a surprise for you." She said.

"What is it?" They both asked curiously at the same time.

"Look behind you." Addison was standing right behind them, wearing a charming smile.

"It'll be an amazing sight to see." He said as he raised his arms in the air.

"Yes, it will," Abigail said as she hugged his neck.

"It's great to see you, my friend." Athens' hands grew sweaty, and his heart rapidly pounded as he envisioned what it would look like while standing on top of the mountain overlooking the city beneath the giant statue.

"It'll be quite exhilarating to actually climb to the top," Abigail suggested.

"Yes, I can't wait!" Addison said as he placed his hands behind his head and stretched from side to side while checking out the scenery.

Athens didn't respond. Climbing to the top wasn't his idea of fun. He picked up a blue flyer off the ground and read it. *The Greatest Show on Earth, including a fun-filled carnival for all ages!* "There's a parade with rides and games. They even have an epic helicopter ride and a super cool kite-flying contest."

"I hope they have blueberry cotton candy. That's my favorite," Abigail said with delight as she pointed up to the hot air balloons.

"Have you ever been in a hot air balloon before?" asked Addison.

"No, and I don't think I ever will," Athens responded. "I'm not a big fan of heights." Athens looked at the Ferris wheel. No way was he ever going to ride one.

"I've been on plenty of Ferris wheels, and they're a lot of fun. You can see everything for miles away when you're sitting up so high. It's like sitting on top of the world." Abigail said as she twirled her hair around her finger.

Eliza shook her angelic head. "I'm sorry, but there's no time to waste. Your nap in the forest has cost you time that you have to make up now. However, I'm glad everyone's in great shape for the hike because it will definitely take a lot out of you. The mountain range is very high, and the air is thin up there. I think we should get going now," she said.

In truth, Athens had a fear of heights. Deep down inside, he knew that facing his fear was the only way to overcome it. Abigail gave him a sympathetic look and asked Eliza, "Is there anything we can do to help Athens overcome his fear of heights?"

Eliza looked into Athens' eyes. "There are many ways to overcome fear. One way is not to think about what you are doing, focus on something else, and do it. Imagine something you'd love to do and envision yourself doing it. Singing is a great way to distract yourself from fear. It's believed that music is the bridge between heaven and earth."

"Think of someone who could cheer you up and pretend like you're doing it for them," Abigail added.

"Another way is to imagine that you're rescuing someone from danger, and their life depends on it. Better yet, take long, deep breaths while focusing on your nose and mouth. Breathe in through your nose and exhale out of your mouth," Addison suggested as they walked and talked along the way.

Abigail exhaled. "Believe in yourself. Tell yourself that you can do it. Say it out loud. Most importantly, pray and talk to God."

"Ask Him to strengthen you and give you more faith and courage. He knows you can't do it alone." Eliza said.

"That's something my mom would say," Athens said.

"Never give doubt, worries, or fear the chance to creep into your mind and ruin your thoughts," Addison added.

Athens suddenly had a plan for overcoming his fear. "Thanks, everybody. I've got it! I need to put on the armor of God. Climbing to the top will strengthen my mind, my body, and my spirit. If I push myself and reach beyond my own limits, I believe God will protect me from the inside out. It isn't going to be easy, but I know with His help, I can do anything!"

"You're totally right." Abigail said, nodding her head.

"We may let ourselves down, and others may let us down too, but I can promise you the King of Kings will never let us down," Athens realized he needed to follow God's plan and not his own. He had nothing to lose but everything to gain. This was his opportunity to free himself from his fear of heights.

"The truth is that everybody is afraid of something. Some people will never admit their fears, while other people let their fear consume them, keeping them from living the best life ever. Everyone's fears are different. It's best to face your fear with courage and try to overcome it." Eliza explained.

"I'm afraid of the dark," Abigail admitted.

"I'm claustrophobic," Addison said under his breath.

"Dude, what is that?" Athens asked with a puzzled look on his face. "I start to feel anxious, and I can't breathe when I get into small tight spaces. Anyway, not to change the subject, but getting to experience one of the greatest wonders of the world will be pretty amazing." Addison said while staring off into space.

Suddenly, all the blood drained from Athens' face. He became filled with fear at the thought of climbing to the top of the mountain.

"Anyone can conquer their fear. You can do it. I believe in you!" Abigail said as she tried to cheer him up with her smile.

Eliza put her hand on his shoulder and quickly reminded him of his identity. "It's by faith that you have taken steps forward to trust God, knowing that you have been righteously chosen," she leaned in close, adding a bit of hope and encouragement. "You've already proven that you have faith like Daniel in the lion's den."

Abigail turned to Addison and asked. "Have you ever heard of Daniel and the lion's den?"

"No, but I know that fear can stop anyone from moving forward." He replied.

"No harm came to Daniel after the king's men had him thrown into a pit with ferocious lions. God sent His angel in the den and protected Daniel from the mouths of the lions, just like he did for us in the field of lions in the Valley of the Kings. Remember?"

"What do you believe faith is?" Addison asked.

Abigail appeared to be thinking this over when Eliza jumped in. "Faith is believing in something you hope for but cannot see. It's like the wind, you can't see it, but you can feel it and see what it does. If you have faith even as small as a mustard seed, you can move mountains." She turned to Athens. "Take the armor pieces, for example. Did you really know that they existed?"

"No, but I dreamed that they did, and when I heard the voice of God, I knew it was Him. Now I'm walking by faith, living out my dream."

"Excellent choice," she said.

"When I received the shoes in the fire, it took faith to move forward and step into the flames."

"Yes, just like it did for Shadrach, Meshach, and Abednego."

"Who on earth is that?" Abigail inquired.

"Three Hebrew friends of Daniel from the Bible who were thrown into a fiery furnace for not bowing down to worship King Nebuchadnezzar of Babylon. They didn't get burned up because God was in the fire with them. Not one hair on their heads was harmed. Their clothes didn't even smell like smoke. I know God will be with you too," Eliza smiled as she looked up into heaven.

"That's incredible. I'd like to meet them someday," Athens said.

"Hey, look over there." Addison pointed to a billboard. There was a picture of *Sugar Loaf Mountain*. There are hundreds of acres of fields that local farmers use to grow sugar beets and sugarcane. They supply much of the Nation's sugar needs right here. They sell loaves, cubes, and granules in the marketplace."

"I think it would be a cool place to visit, maybe even try some sugar," Abigail smiled.

"If we hurry, we can stop by Sugar Loaf mountain since we're headed in that direction. I know how much you love sweets, so I wouldn't want to deprive you of this once-in-a-lifetime opportunity." Athens said.

A few small bees began following them. A buzzing noise was in Addison's ear. He swatted at the curious bee. "I think the bees are following us. They must love sugar too." While passing by some bushes, a loud humming noise came from behind them. Addison turned his head. "Wow, look at that!" A large swarm of bees the size of a bus came flying past them. "Oh man, that's crazy!"

"That's definitely not something you see every day, I wonder where they're going?" Athens said while watching in amazement as the bees fled into a nearby field with cows and horses.

"Do you wanna know something else that's incredible? I heard about these two famous cows that were born with the number seven on their foreheads. It's believed to be a prophetic sign from God. Maybe we can stop to see them. I think they're somewhere around here." Addison mentioned.

"Maybe the bees are a sign. What do you think it could mean?" Abigail asked.

"I don't know about the bees, but I do know a cool story about the cows," Addison replied.

"Please do tell," Abigail said as they continued walking.

"Long ago, it was written in the stars that a young man" named Joseph would become a ruler over Egypt."

Abigail's eyes lit up. "We just came from there."

"This Joseph was the son of Jacob, who was the son of Isaac, who was the son of Abraham. Joseph had eleven brothers. But Joseph was the one blessed to interpret dreams. His brothers were jealous of him because their father favored him the most."

"That's a whole lot of brothers," Natalie twittered while shaking her tail feathers.

"The breastplate Athens is carrying came from their family line of priests, known as the Tribe of Israel." Addison pointed to the unique names and precious stones on the breastplate. "Joseph dreamed that someday his brothers would bow down before him. So, they threw him into a deep pit that he couldn't escape from, and they tore up his special coat of many colors that his father had given him and then they told their father that Joseph must have been killed by a wild animal.

Later, his brothers changed their minds about leaving him in the pit to die and sold him into slavery to a caravan of traders. Many years later, God used Joseph to save Egypt from a horrible famine. The Pharaoh of Egypt kept having the same dream repeatedly, and no one could tell him what it meant until Joseph came along. He explained Pharaoh's dream to him and told him that there were fourteen cows in his dream, seven good healthy fat cows, and seven sickly skinny cows all out in the fields. The cows represented fourteen years of crops. The first seven years represented growth and prosperity with an abundance of wheat and grain to harvest and store up for the seven years to follow, which he described as full of pestilence, drought, and famine that would lead to much death. Pharaoh appointed Joseph to be second in command to rule over Egypt, ensuring there would be plenty of food stored up for the people so that no one would starve during the seven years of famine."

Addison pulled a long piece of grass out of the ground and chewed on the end of it while talking. "It's believed that the days ahead will be a repeat of what happened in Egypt. There were seven years of feast and seven years of famine in the land. The two cows that have the number seven on their heads were born on September 25, 2014, the opening day of the Shemitah—which is a Jewish holiday that represents a resting period of the land after seven years of harvest, according to Jewish customs."

"That's very interesting. I hope we'll be living in one of the King's mansions when that happens," Abigail remarked.

Approaching the mountain, they stood in awe of its enormous size. Athens wasn't sure where to begin. He was hoping Eliza would guide them, but she was needed elsewhere on a different heavenly mission.

Abigail tugged on Athens' shirt. When he turned around, he saw a cute little old man wearing a straw hat standing beneath an umbrella on the street corner next to his vending cart selling sugar loaves. Behind the little old man was a herd of deer watching as they approached.

"Ola," the little old man said as he extended his hand and offered Athens a sugar loaf. "Here you go, try some of my sugar. It's the finest in the land."

"It's made from local sugar beets. It's very sweet and good to eat." He told them the story of how the mountain got its name while Abigail ate bite after bite of the sugar loaf. Athens stared at her.

Abigail's cheeks turned cherry red. "Oops, sorry." She broke pieces off the loaf and gave some to her friends. "After all, that's what friends are for," she added.

Addison smiled and took a bite of the sugar loaf. "We're on our way to the top of the monument. Can you please tell us the best way to get there?" he asked the little old man wearing the straw hat. The man pointed them in the direction to the far east side of the mountain.

"Thank you, Sir. We have to go now," Athens said as they walked away. A bit hesitant, walking toward the mountain, the fear of climbing began to sink in again. Athens' face turned as white as a ghost. Addison gripped his shoulder. "Keep walking by faith, my friend. Don't look back."

"When you get to the top, you won't believe the view. It's spectacular!" yelled the little old man.

"I believe in you," Abigail whispered. "It's going to be amazing." She said as she faced the mountain.

Athens silently prayed a simple prayer inside his head before venturing up the side of the mountain. A circle of clouds formed and expanded across the sky, passing over their heads. They realized a storm was brewing. Abigail held her arms above her head.

"This isn't good." A light mist began to fall on their faces as they looked up into the heavens to see what was happening. The mist quickly turned into a light sprinkle that turned into a drizzle which turned into a gentle rain. Before they knew it, they were standing in the thick of it as the rain came pouring down on top of them.

"Let's find shelter," Abigail yelled over the roaring rain.

"This is no ordinary rain." It took a turn for the worst and turned into a massive hailstorm. "Look out! Those are no ordinary hailstones either," Addison shouted. The giant-sized balls of ice pounded the ground, crushing everything in sight. Each one looked like it could have easily weighed a hundred pounds judging by the size of the imprints that it left on the earth.

"Run for your lives!" Athens yelled. Searching high and low, hoping to escape the fury of the hailstorm, they found shelter in a crevasse along the side of the mountain. A curious nighthawk flew in after them and perched herself on a ledge inside the dark cave. Thunder and lightning continued crackling in the sky, so they squeezed in closer to avoid the dangers of the storm. Addison covered his ears. He hated the loud noise of the thunder. Without warning, the mountain rocks began to shake and rumble. The violent hailstorm caused an avalanche. The rocks crumbled and turned into rubble, barricading them inside the mountain. "No one panic. I'm sure there's another way out," Athens exclaimed as he put his hands on top of his head. The rock walls were built up all around them, closing them in. Mysterious noises were coming from within the walls.

"I'm feeling a little claustrophobic. I don't like being trapped or crowded," Addison's voice cracked.

"I don't like being squashed into small dark places either. It makes me feel panicky and anxious," Abigail's bottom lip quivered as she reached out to grab ahold of Athens arm. Athens knew he had to think of something quick before the two of them went into complete meltdown mode. "We all need enough faith to move mountains. Don't forget, we're here to find the Shield of Faith, aren't we? Don't let a little dark space paralyze your thoughts. Think positive thoughts. Let's sing a song," he suggested. "Abigail, you lead."

Abigail was quiet for a moment. "Seriously?"

"Yeah, I think it will help." he said.

She bit her lip, then lowered her hand away from her mouth and sang. Her soft, soothing voice carried over to the others. Their spirits moved together as one as they sang, standing side by side. Feeling more confident, Abigail let go of Athens' arm and leaned against a wall that slowly began to move. Unsure of her footing and trying her best not to fall, she pushed up against a wall. It unexpectedly opened into a secret passage leading into an underground tunnel.

"Stay close," Abigail cried. "I can't see a thing."

"Don't worry, I'm here," Athens said.

A golden menorah light with seven candles mysteriously appeared on a ledge in the darkness where they were standing. Addison picked it up to have a look around before Athens could open his backpack to get his globe. The sweet little nighthawk followed closely behind and stared at Abigail with her keen, sharp eyes when she decided to speak. "I'm sorry for the intrusion, but I got scared. I can't find my family, and I'm afraid because the storm is so loud. I'm Natalie, by the way."

Abigail glanced her way, and triple blinked her eyes. "You can speak? My name is Abbi, girl. I mean, Abigail," she said with a quiver in her voice. Natalie cracked a smile. Athens smiled as well when he glanced over at Addison, who wore a stunned expression.

Addison looked at Abigail, Natalie, and then Athens with raised eyebrows. "Aren't either one of you shocked?"

Athens laughed. "You know, Natalie isn't the first talking animal we've come across, and I'm sure she won't be the last." Addison scratched the back of his head.

"What happened to your family?" Abigail asked.

Natalie looked away and then softly spoke. "My family didn't want to listen to me when I told them about the massive storm. They stayed home, but I decided to go. Now more than ever, I miss my great-grandpa's big hugs, his funny stories, and my Yia Yia's treehouse garden."

"I'm so sorry, I'm sure the storm will be over soon, and we'll find a way out, somehow." Abigail said, petting her.

"This is bizarre weather we're having here." Athens said as Natalie perched on his shoulder.

"I can tell there's something special about you, but I can't quite put my bill on it." She perked up and put her beak close to his cheek. "What brings you to Brazil? Are you here for the festivities? We have the greatest carnival on earth where everything comes to life right on the streets, like magic. My favorite is the cupcake competition. I get the breadcrumbs right off the table, and believe me, they're delicious," she tweeted.

"I'd love to have one of those right about now. I'm so hungry I could eat an elephant." Abigail said.

Athens chuckled. "If you must know the truth, we're on a global mission. We're in search of a sacred armor piece called the Shield of Faith."

"Once we find it, we'll continue on our journey until we get to the land of milk and honey in Israel to meet the King. Would you like to come with us? We'd love to have your perspective from a bird's-eye view." Abigail giggled.

"I've never been on an adventure before, but maybe it would be good for me." After thinking it over for a bit, Natalie responded. "Sure, count me in, that is, if we ever get out of here."

Abigail noticed a glum look on Addison's face and asked if everything was okay. Addison expelled a deep breath. "Well, if you really want to know the truth, I don't have a family to speak of. That's why I'm on my way to Israel. I want to find my Jewish roots."

"I sort of know how you feel. I lost my parents when I was very young, so I've lived with my grandmother up until now."

"I'm so sorry for your losses, I can't imagine how you must feel, but I do understand the desire to want to be with family." Athens closed his eyes and imagined what it would be like living in the King's mansion with his family and friends. How magnificent would it be to walk down the streets of gold and live a life free from fear, worry, and pain?" Everyone stood silent just long enough to hear music coming up from beneath their feet.
The ground rumbled, and their feet vibrated as the music grew louder and louder.

"What could that be," Natalie twittered?

It was the most beautiful sound they had ever heard. Curious about the music and wondering where it was coming from, Athens carefully moved forward listening closely, while following the sound of the music, not knowing where it would lead them.

"Stay close behind me." He said. The instruments sounded magical. The ribbons of harps, strings, and violins played magnificently together.

Natalie got anxious and flew ahead. "Follow me." She said. They climbed over gigantic rocks and squeezed between two boulders with barely enough room to spare.

"Where are we?" Abigail inquired. No-one answered.

The stone walls were dark and wet, and the ground was slippery, causing them to slip and slide. One of them tumbled and hit the ground, then they all fell one on top of another like a pile of bowling pins. Getting up was no easy task. The walls were nearly impossible to hang on to inside the cavern.

Finally, they stood up as one accord and pushed their way through to gain access to the other side. The walls were still sweating and dripping with water and led to a little stream that fed into a deep pool of glowing water. The pool was so vibrant and refreshing. It appeared to be living water.

"What do you think the water is used for?" Addison said.

No one answered. Suddenly, candles mysteriously lit up the entire room. A knight in shining armor stood brightly in the corner behind a small altar. Athens' eyes widened.

He'd never seen anything like it before. It was extraordinary. He knew in an instant that the shield must be somewhere nearby. He knelt at the altar to pray while Natalie sat next to him, fluffing her feathers.

Athens lifted his eyes… Low and behold, he saw the shield's reflection in her eyes glistening in the dark.

Abigail and Addison were still looking around in disbelief, wondering what they had stumbled onto, when Athens got up and moved toward the shield. His eyes stared at the four images on it as if being drawn to them. His curious mind led him to rub the smooth polished images with his fingertips. A face of a man, a lion's head, an ox, and an eagle were embossed on the shield. Like a reflection from heaven, Eliza magically appeared.

"Athens, you've found the shield, congratulations! The images you're touching are symbols of God. Each one has great meaning; the lion represents supreme strength like a king, the man - like the Son of God having wisdom, the Ox - is like a lowly servant, the eagle is elevated and means – heavenliness and divinity. Your faith has brought you here, and now it's time to take up the shield and head to the top of the mountain to conquer your fear."

She opened a passageway and led them to the top of the mountain where Christ The Redeemer's giant statue was positioned. "I can do this, I got this." Athens felt the urgency to pray. Please remove my fear and give me more faith and courage. Lord of Lords and King of Kings. I need peace in my heart and mind. He felt a sudden breeze of cool fresh air rush across his face. He took in a deep breath that stirred up his faith and courage.

Then he inched his way to the edge and looked out over the entire countryside. His insides were shaking. He realized how high up it was and took another deep breath. A wave of energy flowed through him, giving him the ability to conquer his fear. His friends rushed over. Judging by the look on his face, they realized he had conquered his fear. "You did it, and you helped us overcome our fears too." Abigail cheered.

"Thanks, man," Addison patted him on the back.

Athens grinned from ear to ear. He raised both hands toward heaven and shouted from the edge of the mountain, "I can do all things through Jesus Christ who strengthens me!"

Addison's lips parted, "Who is this Jesus you're talking about? I don't know Him."

"This great monument that we are standing under is of Jesus Christ. He is the Son of God and the Son of man. He came into the world in human form to save us from our sins over 2,000 years ago and walked in the flesh. Someday, the whole world will know Him and call Him by name. To this day, He performs miracles and changes lives. His Spirit lives inside of us." Athens was strengthened and filled with the anointing powers of Jesus. "Whosoever believes, and Trusts in Him will have the gift of eternal life. Our job as believers is to share the message of hope, love, and forgiveness, telling others about His love and mercy. We're all sinners, and we needed a Savior to forgive us from our sins."

"What is sin?" Addison asked.

Athens shifted his weight from one foot to the other and looked at Abigail, then turned to Addison.

How was he supposed to answer? Before long, he spoke. "Sin is when you go against God — doing things you know you shouldn't do like stealing, lying, or cheating. Hurting people on purpose is a sin. If you don't tell the truth, you are deceiving yourself and others. God doesn't like it when we choose to do the wrong things. It causes our relationship to be in a bad place. There are consequences for making bad choices. It may not happen right away, but everything eventually comes back full circle."

Athens drew a circle on the ground with his finger, then looked up intently. "God wrote the law of the Ten Commandments for us to obey, but it was too hard to follow, so He chose to send His only Son into the world to help us. Jesus paid the price for our sins with His life and shed His blood on the cross so that someday when we die, we get to go to heaven."

Next, Athens drew a cross in the dirt. Abigail kneeled beside him to listen. "Those who accept the Truth about God's Son and ask Him to come into their lives will be forgiven and inherit the kingdom of heaven."

Eliza chimed in. "God can fill our hearts with his love. It's also a privilege to get to go to heaven. Someday, every knee will bend, and every head will bow before the throne of God! Those who deny Him and plot to do evil will not inherit God's Kingdom but instead will go to a place called Sheol, also known as Hades or hell. It's a dark place where there will be wailing and gnashing of teeth. A pit of fire and brimstone will burn for all eternity.

There is no escaping it." Athens' said.

"I don't want to go there," Addison said, wiping the sweat from his brow. "It sounds horrific."

Athens nodded his head to agree. "That's why it's so important to use self-control and do the right thing. Having the Belt of Truth, the Breastplate of Righteousness, and the Gospel Shoes of Peace helps me to share the good news and helps me to be a good example for others to follow. All you have to do is ask Him for forgiveness and turn away from sin, then do your best to obey His commandments. And share the truth with others about what you've learned. <u>Once we admit the Truth, that we are sinners and believe in our hearts that Jesus came into the world and died for our sins, and confess it with our lips, then we are saved from God's wrath to come.</u>"

"Can we pray and ask Him right now?" Abigail asked while chewing her fingernails.

"Yes, let's ask Him now," Addison pleaded.

"Sure, there's no time like the present." They joined hands. "Lord Jesus, Lord of lords and King of Kings, the Son of the everlasting God, please come into our lives and fill our hearts with love. Forgive us for our sins. Fill us with Your everlasting hope, love, and mercy. Reveal Yourself to us in a mighty way so that we will do Your will and not our own. Thank you for loving us unconditionally and for helping us overcome our fears, doubts, and worries. In Jesus Holy name, Amen." The three of them looked up into the sky and stared into the heavens in awe. Eliza's heart was bursting with joy as she stretched out her hands.
She looked at Abigail and noticed her necklace. "The necklace you are wearing is a symbol of Jesus showing His love for you through the cross."

"Wow, you're right. I'm so blessed, thank you!"

Eliza gave her a radiant smile before fading out. Then Athens led them to the hidden rock. Standing back to back with their arms linked together, Natalie perched herself on Athens' shoulder. Without hesitating, he spoke the words; and they all disappeared without a trace.

Fun Facts:

- The two cows with the number 7 on their heads are likened to the two cows in Pharaoh's dream. One was born in Israel, and one was born in the United States on the same day. See author Jonathan Cahn's story about their prophetic meaning.

- Sugar Loaf Mountain is in Brazil. Sugar beets supply most of their nation's sugar needs.

- There are many amazing prophetic stories connecting Joseph to Jesus in the scriptures.

- 100-pound sized hailstones are mentioned in the last book of the Bible in Revelation 16:21.

- The four emblems on the shield have true meaning from the Bible. See Ezekiel 1:10 & Revelation 4:6.

- Athens really has a fear of heights. He prays, seeking God's love, wisdom, and direction concerning all things in his daily walk with Christ.

- My daughter Diona and my son-in-law saw a swarm of bees the size of a bus near Zephyr-hills, Florida.

- Christ The Redeemer is one of the seven wonders of the world located in Rio de Janeiro, Brazil.

- Look on page 170 to learn more about the shield.

Significance of the two Shemitah calves:
FACT 2. Represent 14 cows in Pharoah's dream

CHAPTER 5

DEFEATING THE ENEMY

HELMET OF SALVATION

Deception Island, Antarctica

Athens and his friends appeared, dressed in warm pants and winter coats, ready to take on the world when Eliza entered the atmosphere like a brilliant light.

"There's no other place on Earth quite like the South Pole. It's the coldest and darkest place in the world. Beyond the icebergs and freezing snowy weather are many hidden treasures that have been kept secret until now. You'll soon discover how this volcanic island got its name. It's dark nearly six months out of the year here in Antarctica."

Abigail shivered while rubbing her nose. "Wait! What? I'm glad we won't be here that long."

"Living in darkness with barely any light for months at a time would feel like torture," Natalie tweeted as her feathers shook in the frigid cold air.

"I can't even imagine living in darkness every day. That would be depressing to me," Addison shook his head and put his hands in his pockets. Athens looked around. He was curious about some strange-looking mossy weeds growing on the ground and wondered if it was edible. He looked at Eliza as if asking her the question with his eyes.

"Nothing much grows here, besides Pearlwort and hair grass plants, because of the freezing temperatures," she said. "Not many people live here for that very reason. The mountainside has deep dredges that were formed by spewing hot lava but for decades, not a single ounce of volcanic activity has been found on the island until now. Something very unusual is happening. There's a supermassive, ghostly black hole that keeps spreading throughout the region. No one knows where it came from or why it's here. Its existence can't be explained. Some people believe that the black hole was caused by something from outer space, called kryptonite matter, which fell from the sky, forming a big black hole. Rumor has it that it could be a portal used by fallen angels and their offspring to travel back and forth from one dimension to another, allowing evil activity to wreak havoc on our great planet Earth."

"That sounds crazy, but my dad used to tell me stories about the Nephillim creatures, who are the offspring of the fallen angels. I hope we don't run into any of them while we're here."

"Look over there, sled mushers with their dogs. They appear to be getting ready for a race. It would be fun to watch them run through the sleet and snow, racing to the finish line." Abigail said, rubbing her hands together to keep warm.

"Only the best of the best win. The mushers must have total concentration if they want to succeed. The dogs are amazing animals. They work hard as a team and are completely obedient and devoted to their masters." Athens watched as they lined up to race. "I read it in one of my books back home."

Eliza quickly chimed in, "The mushers must remain clear-minded, light-hearted, and quick on their feet. Staying focused is crucial to the task. In the same way, Athens must be in complete union with God's will if he plans on finishing the quest on time." She turned and gave Abigail a nudge, knowing she can be a distraction for him at times. Abigail's check turned flush.

They walked along the freezing shoreline, looking for clues on where to find the helmet, when a human-sized curious penguin waddled over and took one look at them and blurted out, "My word, you're a couple of handsome gems, she said to Athens and Addison. Your eyes are as bright as the morning sun and twinkle like the evening stars, and your hair is as shiny as a midsummer eve. I think I'm falling in love already. May I add the girls are as lovely as the light on a moonlit sky."

Eliza's blue eyes twinkled while Athens and Abigail were blushing and didn't quite know what to say. But Addison was smiling from ear to ear, soaking it all in. A gorgeous young lady wearing an Eskimo coat and gloves approached them from the ocean bank and asked in a calm, soothing voice, "What gives us the honor of your presence? My name is Diona Ardearest."

"I'm the islander hostess, and this is Penelope, my friend." Penelope quickly tried to hide her face behind Diona. She seemed a little embarrassed about being too outspoken. After everyone introduced themselves, Athens was eager to share the good news with them. But Abigail spoke first. "How on earth did you get to be so big?" she asked. "You're ginormous for a penguin if you don't mind me saying so."

"I was about to ask the same thing." Natalie chirped as her little beak chattered from the cold.

Penelope stood tall and proud, then replied, "I inherited my prehistoric genes from my ancestors' of long ago. They were the same monumental size as me. My family comes in all different shapes, colors, and sizes. I love them all. I also love ice-sculpting with my beak, in case you wanted to know. It's very satisfying, except for when my tongue gets stuck to the ice. That part really hurts. She chuckled. But honestly, there are some perks to being ginormous. For instance, being this tall helps me to see from far away, and it's especially nice when I'm skating on the ice or when I'm about to dive into the ocean to catch some fish. Do you all like to fish? Have you ever seen a crucifix catfish before?" she asked, but before anyone could answer, she continued. "I happen to have some over here. Come take a look."

When Penelope took a breath, Diona took over the conversation. "Every year, fishermen come from all over the world to enter the great fishing competition. Last year my Papou, I mean my grandpa, won the grand prize for catching the most exotic and largest crucifix catfish ever, and he was only in a small canoe."

The crucifix catfish bones were laid out on the snow and were like nothing they had ever seen before.
The skull's jagged edges were thick in the middle.
You could almost see a face etched out of the top-center portion. The arms were stretched out on both sides and the legs aimed down, like the image of Jesus on the cross." Penelope picked up the bones and shook them. They stared in fascination. "That's so cool," Abigail responded.

"When you shake the bones and hear a rattle in the breastplate, it will bring you good luck," Penelope added.

"What an extraordinary bone structure. It's ingenious. We just came from Brazil, where Christ Our Redeemer Monument is located. This is an amazing confirmation of His existence," Addison said in a high-pitched voice. "We're in search of a unique helmet that belongs to the great King Elohim."

"What helmet, and who is King Elohim?" Diona asked while posing with her hands on her hips.

"King Elohim is the King from my dream. I've been sent here on this quest to find the Truth and to share the good news about Him with others. The Helmet of Salvation has supernatural powers that were crafted in the heavenly realms. It's one of six armor pieces that I need, and so far, I have found four of them." Athens said.

"We'll soon be on the other side of the world in America, searching for the Sword of the Spirit in a place called Yosemite National Park, California," Abigail added.

"All the armor pieces work together like magic to creates supernatural elements of protection to defeat evil.

Once I find all of them and take them to the King of Israel, we will become heirs to His throne and inherit the gift of Eternal Life. It will forever change our lives. I have to find the helmet before it's too late. Do you happen to know where I can find it?" Athens asked with a bit of hope in his eyes.

Diona and Penelope looked at each other in wonder as their eyes widened. Athens was waiting for a response when Diona looked at him with her piercing brown eyes and said, "My Papou, I mean my grandpa, just shared a story with us a few days ago. It stuck out in my mind because he mentioned something about an old volcano with dark treasures, a map, and a supernatural helmet. My Papou is Greek and wants to make sure that his stories and traditions are passed down from generation to generation, keeping them alive for all the ages to come. He's always telling us new stories and often repeats the old ones. I didn't believe there was much truth to them until now. We just thought they were old wise tales and enjoyed listening to them. I remember him telling us about the helmet's significance and how it can change the way people think and behave. He spoke of a dark cave and how it could play tricks on people's minds."

Eliza spoke up and raised her hands. "The helmet has the power to protect a person's mind from deceptive thoughts. Knowing the truth and seeing the difference between right and wrong is wonderful, but it's not enough to know what is right and wrong. The power comes from doing the right thing, even when it costs you something. Even if that something is your life."

Athens' heart pounded rapidly. He'd rather keep his life then lose it.

"If you trust your instincts and have faith in Jesus, you will have hope when all hope is lost," Abigail said while clasping her hands together, still trying to get warm.

"I have to be completely honest with you," Diona explained. "Anyone brave enough to go there must first be aware of the dangers."

"There are two kinds of wars. The physical and the spiritual. Both are battles between light and dark, good and evil. It's up to you to figure out which is which." Eliza said.

"By the way, I can get my Papou's map for you, if that will help."

"That would be great," Athens replied. "Oh, wait," I have my 3D onyx globe." He pulled it out of his backpack to get a glimpse of the cave, but it didn't give him the vision he wanted. "I don't understand why it's not showing me the inside of the cave." Instead, an image of heaven appeared. They stood in awe of its grand beauty. "I guess we need the map after all." He said.

Diona spoke. "I'll meet you in town and give it to you in an hour, but first, I need to give you a few tips. Get on your knees and pray. Many Kings and Noblemen have gone astray, worshiping such idols found in the caves. Many have been led to their doom."

"Don't let this happen to you," Penelope's beak chattered.

"The dark cave's secret treasures carried a curse hidden deep within the belly of the Earth. The chambers are deadly. They hold enchanting powers that will lead you to your death if you disturb the creatures of the underground world." Eliza uttered.

"Oh man," Natalie gasped as her little eyes popped open.

"Deceitful, nasty, Nephillim lurk about, searching for souls to devour. They'll use mind control to influence your thoughts," Diona whispered, looking over her shoulder. "Once their unclean spirits have crept into a person's mind, it's hard to get them out."

"That's why you must guard your mind, so your thoughts will be protected. Never allow your thoughts to turn against you, causing doubt, fear, worry, or anxiety. It's a trick they use to rob you of your own will and peace of mind. If you allow them to control your thoughts, your own beliefs will disappear forever, and you will become a part of their dark, evil, deceptive world," Eliza said.

"Don't be deceived, or they could own you forever," Penelope pleaded as she shook her flippers and tail feathers.

"I remember my father telling me stories about the Nephillim creatures from one of his ancient texts called *The Book of Enoch*. They're fearsome freaky creatures," Athens said.

"The name Deception Island is just that. It's in the shape of a U, and it draws unsuspecting souls to it like a magnet. Its hidden treasures and mystical powers lie within the volcano walls. People come searching for riches. Scientists come searching for portals to other worldly realms. But they never leave the island the same way they came, if they leave at all. Most disappear and are never seen again," Penelope replied.

Natalie was perched on Addison's should now. They both stood there like frozen statues listening to every word.

"They will trick you, and lie to you to get you to go astray," Diona shivered.

"I'm terrified," Natalie's little voice shrieked.

"Stay close. I'll protect you," Addison said.

"My Papou says thousands of souls are hidden in the bowels of the volcano, awaiting judgment day." Diona said while shuffling her feet in the snow.

"Wow, that's scary. I don't mean to sound dumb, but what are Nephillim?" Natalie asked as her voice screeched and her beak chattered with fear.

"They're bad celestial spirits. Truly deceitful, horrible, wicked beings. The Nephillim are plotting to take over the world and change the lives of everyone we know. They're cloning themselves as we speak to carry out evil deeds. They are the lords of sin." Penelope admitted.

"They must be stopped!" Athens insisted. "According to my dad, they can transform themselves into almost anything. Don't be fooled by their appearances and outwardly beauty. It's a disguise."

Eliza gave them one final alert. "You will encounter many marvelous treasures in the cave, but don't be deceived by their beauty, for it's equal to their trouble. Whatever you do, don't touch them. Only get the helmet. The Nephillim will try to use their powers to keep you from leaving. They're hoping you'll spend the rest of your life in eternal flames of torment and fire along with them."

Abigail's eyes grew wide with fear as she listened.

"Be strong, be brave, be alert, and above all else, use self-control. This isn't just any ordinary cave. The moment you let any of its enchanting powers seep into your minds, it's over," Diona said.

"Oh, dear," Abigail pleaded. "This may be a problem for me." She put her hands to her cheeks and stared at the ground.

"Their power and beauty will make it nearly impossible for you to turn away from them. Only a true believer can overcome the obstacles put before him, no matter what it takes. The secret is to keep your eyes centered on the truth and protect your heart, mind, and body, so that you can continue to fight for the prize ahead and not get caught up in the treasures immediately in front of you," Eliza made a golden key appear in her hands and then in a flash she made it disappear.

"Remember, do not be overtaken by the angels of darkness. They'll appear as a beautiful light, but their true identity will horrify you. They're nothing like Eliza, whose grace and beauty are beyond compare. Her spirit is magnified by her radiant glow which reflects the heavens above," Penelope clapped her fins together.

Eliza was forbidden to go into the cave to help Athens, so she gave him a menorah light to help guide them in the dark. "Don't forget, I have the globe that my parents gave me." He handed the light stand to Abigail.

"At least now, I'm somewhat armed," Abigail said with an exalted laugh.

After hearing about the Nephillim, Addison and Natalie preferred to stay behind with Diona and Penelope. Athens didn't want to risk their lives anyway.

Eliza moved in closer. "The best thing we can do for Athens and Abigail is to pray for them and hope that they'll escape the traps and snares that have been set before them." Eliza turned back towards Athens. She held a unique precious stone carved into the shape of a gigantic egg called the stone of Eilat. "This came from King Solomon's Mine. It's the only one of its kind. You must put it in the place of the helmet when the time is right when the helmet is presented to you. This will be a true test of your character. To be able to do God's will and not your own desire will be the ultimate test."

She handed Athens the precious stone of Eilat, assuring him of its importance. She hoped he wouldn't want to keep it for himself and would choose to put it in its rightful place.

"I hope you return safe and sound so you can join us later this evening," Penelope gave Athens a giant hug, squeezing him tight, lifting him up off the ground.

"Umm, I hope so too, you can let go of me now." Athens said with a chuckle.

Diona gave a peaceful smile. "Our doors are always open for God's blessings to cover us from the temptations of the island and keep us safe from falling into the hands of the evil ones. With that being said, I'll go get my Papou's map now." Everyone else headed over to see the ice-sculpting exhibit in town.

When Diona returned, she gave Abigail the map. Athens took another look into his globe, hoping to catch a glimpse of what was up ahead, but it wouldn't reveal anything to him. He couldn't understand why it wasn't working the way he wanted it to.

"It's not a crystal ball," Eliza pleaded. "It reveals heaven, so you can see what you have to look forward to and will strengthen you for the tasks ahead. You can also use it as a way to reflect where you've been. We may not always get what we want, but God always gives what we need."

Athens was disappointed by her answer but accepted the truth.

"By the way, I thought you should know; there's a total lunar eclipse, called a Super Blood Wolf Moon, tonight. It's believed that something very unusual will happen around midnight," Diona remarked as she looked up into the dark sky.

"Yes, it's a natural phenomenon that occurs when the sun, earth, and moon are all three in total alignment," Eliza twirled her hands together in the shape of a ball and created a miniature moonbeam and released it into the atmosphere. They watched as it floated away.

"Yes, it's an extremely rare occurrence," Diona said while gazing at the moonbeam.

"It's a sign from God that something big is about to happen," Athens said as his eyes peered up to heaven.

"Maybe it's your lucky day," Addison suggested.

"No luck needed," Athens replied. "This is our destiny by divine appointment. God is at work on our behalf."

They stood for a moment gazing up at the mountain smoke lingering beneath the moonlit sky before Athens and Abigail departed with the map and headed down a separate path to discover the volcano's secret entrance. They high-stepped it through the thick snow as more flakes fell on their coats and covered their heads in white. A huge rumbling noise broke out. The ground vibrated, throwing them off balance. They fled for cover, hoping to escape the volcano's fury.

"Don't panic. Everything will be okay," Athens motioned to get his globe while entering a dark and dreary cave. Hoping not to disturb anything inside, Abigail used the menorah light to view the map while Athens dug into his backpack. But the light blew out. The air was thick and musty, and it was hard to breathe. They heard a strange noise sweeping through the cave.

A colony of bats flew in from another room. There were thousands of them. "Yikes!" Abigail swatted at the bats with the menorah lamp while ducking her head in fear of getting bitten. "No way!" Athens grabbed the shield instead of the globe and covered their heads with it. He closed his eyes and prayed. "Jesus, please help me and protect us."

A golden aura of light surrounded them in a lit bubble that kept the bats from attacking. The bats circled over their heads and around their bodies, trying to find a way inside the bubble, but they kept bouncing right off the shield. Some of them hit the walls, some of them became mangled as soon as they hit the ground. Athens watched the rest of the bats flee back to wherever they came from while Abigail hid her eyes.

"You can open your eyes now. They're gone."

"We won't be trapped down here forever, will we?" Abigail cried out when she drew blood from chewing on her fingernails. Athens covered their heads and held her hand to calm her while examining the cave further.

The walls sparkled in the dim light. They both rubbed their hands along the rough dark edges of the walls. Abigail felt something hard and jagged protruding from one of the rocks. A sparkling gem fell into her hand as her fingers passed over it. She let go of Athens' hand and got behind him. Some of the other gems were loose and fell out when she touched them. She picked them up and put them in her pockets. Before realizing it, she had plucked out many of the brilliant gems of every shape, size, and color. Her pockets quickly began to fill up. There were layers and layers of diamonds, sparkling sapphires, rubies of fire, and stunning green emeralds that saturated the walls.

Athens stopped mid-step and turned around to see what she was doing. *Had she lost focus? Was she losing her mind? Were the enchanted gems turning into her idol?*

A faint noise trickled through the walls. Athens looked up. Three volcanic tubes appeared to be leading straight up to heaven. *Where had the noise come from?* He followed the tube on his right, leaving Abigail to her own devices.

A reflection came from a wall inside. He squinted his eyes through the darkness. Something strange was

moving around in the dim light. *What was it?*
He stepped in closer to get a better view. It was a series
of glow worms only found in the deepest darkest parts of
the Earth. Athens took a step back and gasped.

What an extraordinary discovery. A secret message was
revealed beneath the layer of rocks that had been etched
into the stone wall out of diamonds: *Behold, the hand of
God. Only one with a pure heart may retrieve the helmet.*
He could hardly believe his own eyes. This was an
incredible find. He looked ahead and could see a brightly
illuminated object in the tube.

Could that be the helmet? Advancing toward it, he
suddenly froze. A still, quiet voice filled his mind. The
helmet will keep your mind clear from deception and
protect your thoughts from ungodly thinking. It will keep
you hidden, so others will not see you said the voice
inside his head. Then he quickly remembered what Eliza
said about replacing the Eilat stone for the helmet. His
life and the lives of many others were depending on it.

This rare precious stone felt extremely heavy as the
beauty of it glistened in his hands. It could make him
rich. *But would he disobey God? Was his willpower to do
the right thing greater than his desire to be rich?* He drew
his hands out to touch the helmet but then hesitated.
Was he having second thoughts? He couldn't reach it. It
was too far away. The helmet began to glimmer and
glow as it ascended from its perch. Suspended in midair,
he watched it slowly come down and land right on top of
his head. He took the Eilat stone, placed it where the
helmet was and put his hands on top of the helmet.
"Thank you, Jesus!"

The dazzling, stones completely lit up the room and encircled his head like a glowing crown of jewels. There was no other helmet like it anywhere on the planet. It fit snugly as though the crown was meant to be his all along. Once it was on his head, every cell in his body tingled, he felt lighter somehow. He glanced down at his torso and let out a little yelp as his body became transparent. He watched as it shimmered, then slowly dissolved. He was invisible. Athens turned around to look for Abigail, but she wasn't there. He could feel the presence of God from within, at the same time sensing evil was not far away. Now he had to find Abigail. *Had she become distracted by the enchanted gemstones?*

"Abigail, where are you?" He whispered while walking through small dark places searching for her. "Oh no," he discovered mounds of skulls and bones piled up as high as the eye could see. He tried not to disturb them when a loud noise erupted from the tube next to him. He headed deeper into the darkest part of the cave. Looking up, he witnessed a blast of shooting stars like a meteor shower moving down into the tube beside him. He stood in shock and watched as flashes and waves of light turned into scary creatures, right before his eyes. The creatures then transformed into beautiful, angelic-like beings as soon as their feet touched the ground.

Wow, Abigail isn't gonna believe this. They no longer appeared as wicked, demonic creatures but were completely disguised. They had to be the Nephillim. Abigail must have heard the noise, too. A second later, she peeked her head around the corner from another tube. Not realizing the creatures had transformed, she became mesmerized and was star-struck by their beauty.

"Come on, stop gawking. They're dangerous and will kill us if they find us here. Let's go before we're trapped down here forever in this dreadful place."

"Athens, is that you?" Abigail's voice shook as she looked around for him. "I can't see you."

Athens grabbed her by the arm and whispered. "I'm wearing the helmet. It's making me invisible."
He squeezed her hand tight. Tiptoeing away, they navigated their way through the dark and dreary cave that led passed a dungeon with countless bodies and skeletons. It was their only way out.

Athens was trying not to look at them as he stepped around some of the bodies. "Don't look at them."
He whispered.

"I'm trying not to," — she said as she tripped over a string. Oh no, her arms flailed into the air. "Whoa."

It released a giant pendulum that swung back and forth like an ax and nearly chopped off Athens' head.
The blood rushed out of his face as the pendulum graced the top of his helmet, knocking it off onto the ground.

"There you are. Now, I can see you. Thank God that thing didn't chop off your head." Abigail said.

Just then, the Nephillim creatures heard Abigail, and they saw Athens too. Their deep dark red eyes glazed over and grew larger than life. Their scary evil faces were like wild beasts. They stretched open their mouths and revealed their nasty fangs and razor-sharp teeth made of iron. Abigail covered her mouth and gasped. The creatures drew back their heads and raced toward them. Abigail leaped into the air like a karate expert kicking her long legs and sent the creatures flying across the room. Gems were falling out of her pockets.

Athens put the helmet back on and head-butted the last of the creatures, knocking them back like a stack of dominos. They didn't know what hit them.

Natalie, the nighthawk, swooped in and helped. She used her beak and talons to poke out their eyes, causing the creatures to fall on their faces in despair. The Earth began to shake and the ground rumbled and quaked. Daggers hanging from the ceiling shook loose. Some of them fell on the Nephillim, giving Abigail and Athens a running start toward the cave entrance.

Athens' feet became hot as the smoldering smoke rose from the cave floor. He pumped his feet faster. The volcano was getting ready to erupt. Abigail's pace slowed as she reached for more jewels, stuffing them in her pockets. *What was she thinking?*

The Earth crept open, and a river of fire and brimstone seeped through the cracks in the ground. The cave entrance was just ahead, but the creatures would probably catch them before they could escape. *What could Athens do?* A brilliant thought entered his mind after he saw ashes and particles floating in the air. He quickly pulled out his long ponytail that was tucked beneath his shirt. This was the secret he'd promised his mother to keep hidden until the appointed time. Even while swimming in the ocean, he'd concealed it by wrapping it up tight in a small bun at the nape of his neck. His eyes gazed around, searching for something to cut it with when he found an old but sharp mining knife sticking up out of the ground. He clutched his hair in one hand and made a fist with the other while holding the knife, then he chopped his hair off with one swoop, leaving only a few strands to keep as a remnant to serve as a reminder of the promise he'd kept to his mother and to God. Athens quickly knelt down and felt the heat on his skin as he lit the hair in his hand on fire. The smell of burnt hair filled the atmosphere. He divided the strands of hair into three sections and spread it across the cave floor to create a smokescreen. He watched as the ashes and smoke drifted upward, filling the cave. Athens needed to warn Abigail.

The river of lava was oozing higher and higher. "Run, Abigail, RUN!" He raced back to get her and held the shield over both their heads to avoid the falling daggers. Passing through the smoke and debris, they began coughing and choking on the thick smoke. Athens was afraid the creatures would escape after them, but more daggers fell from the ceiling and entrapped most of them. Some of the creatures crawled after them grabbing at their ankles. One of the creatures lunged for Abigail, and just missed her after she unloaded the rest of the gems from her pockets causing the creature to stumble. Then a glorious wind blew in and magnified the smoke and debris, blinding the creature. Barely making it out alive, stopping only to take a breath before moving on. The mountain simmered and came to a halt when Natalie flew out of the cave after them. Abigail and Athens hugged when they saw her.

Athens pulled a string from his shirt and twisted the few strands of hair together that he had left and tucked it away so no one would notice it. But Abigail was watching and asked him why he had the long strand of hair. He responded by saying; "I had to keep my promise to God and to my mother. She never allowed me to cut it. She said it would be used to serve God someday. So, I kept it secretly hidden until now. I used it to blind the creatures."

"Wow, that's remarkable. I can't believe you kept it from me all these years," she said with admiration.

"Let's hurry and go tell our friends about the helmet." Natalie twittered. "It's truly a masterpiece." Natalie flew ahead to announce they were coming. When they walked into the town square, all eyes were on them.

"The helmet," Penelope exclaimed. "It's so grandiose!"

"You have it! I can't believe it. It's truly a vision of greatness," Diona cried out.

"How did you escape?" Addison wanted to know.

"With God's help, all things are possible, God will always direct us in the way we are to go if we choose to pay attention. He's never too early, and He's never too late. He's always right on time. So, He's sure to get all the honor and praise that He deserves." Athens spoke as he held the helmet up high for all to see.

The band began to play music as they walked over to the open fire to meet Diona's Papou. She introduced them as honored guests. "Welcome," Papou said as he offered them some hot chocolate. His eyes gazed upon the helmet in amazement. "It's truly a remarkable piece of armor. You are very blessed." Papou added.

"Yes, Sir," Athens responded. A moment later, Athens noticed Abigail had a frown on her face as she lowered her head to her chest. "What's the matter, Abigail?"

"Images of the terrifying creatures keep flashing before my eyes. It's making me feel anxious. I can't get rid of the vision of their iron, razor-sharp teeth? I can almost see them in front of me." She dug her heels into the ground and rubbed her eyes.

Athens gave her the helmet to wear to protect her mind. "Remember to focus on positive thoughts, redirect your thinking." A bright light entered her mind.

"Look, a delicious plate of fresh fish with a bowl of seaweed salad," Penelope said, opening her wide beak.

Athens' mouth watered. He was starving. "It looks delicious," he replied as Diona gave him the largest plate of food. "I hope you like it." She responded.

"I've never had seaweed salad before, but I'm willing to give it a try," he chuckled as Abigail stared at her plate.

"What are you thinking about now, Abigail?" he asked.

"I saw a bright light, then the face of Jesus appeared, now my thoughts have completely changed." She shook her head and took off the helmet, and placed it in Athens' backpack for safekeeping.

Athens remembered to say a quick prayer, thanking God for all their blessings before wiping their plates clean. The moon turned scarlet red as the eclipse began to happen. A moment later, the clouds covered the moon, blocking their view completely.

"I hope the clouds move away soon," Diona moaned. While heading over to the giant telescopes they prayed for the clouds to depart. Before long, the Wolf moon reappeared as it broke through the clouds. "What a vision, the moon is spectacular! It's completely red and so large that you can almost reach out and touch it." Abigail said, dancing beneath the stars and moonlit sky.

"God has truly blessed us tonight," Addison replied as he watched Abigail dancing with a sparkle of moonlight in his eye.

"Athens, can you and your friends stay a bit longer? You have to see the ice-skating performance. Diona has a surprise for you. She's our featured entertainer and wanted to keep it a secret. It's a victory celebration in your honor! No one has ever done what you've done and lived to tell about it," said Penelope.

"Thank you, but we really do need to be going."

Abigail handed Papou his map and thanked him for sharing it with them. "We won't be needing it anymore," she said.

"On second thought, I guess we can stay a little longer." Athens grinned.

They moved over to the arena just as a new song rang out. Stardust fell from heaven and covered their heads as Diona entered the arena. She gracefully glided across the ice. Three small rainbow birds perched on her shoulder. These fabulous birds twittered while whirling above her head. What a lovely vision it was, watching their graceful swoops and swirls in the air. Diona was absolutely breathtaking too. Her arms and legs elegantly swayed back and forth like an angel gently floating by. Then Seven more birds flew in to join her, fluttering about her body, dancing in unison to the sound of the music. A gentle snow began to fall on her nose and her lashes while she danced beneath the moonlight. She began singing as she spun and twirled around in circles. "Snowflakes, snowflakes, lovely little snowflakes." The snowflakes were a wondrous sight. The birds reflection on the ground began shooting radiant beams of brightly colored lights into the sky. Streaks of rainbows danced through the air. Beautiful prisms touched down right in the center of the arena as Diona skated through them. She looked pretty with the lights covering her body. It was a vision of heaven on earth.

"It's like the Aurora Borealis lights in Alaska. It's truly fascinating." Abigail said as they stood in awe, watching the performance.

When the music slowed down, Diona's friends from the village joined her on the ice and formed a single line, then they skated off in every direction creating spectacular moves and jumps with great skill and talent. Everyone clapped and cheered for them.

Athens enjoyed their time together but knew it was time to mush off to the next continent. He wished their new friends farewell and hoped to see them again someday.

Diona and Penelope had handmade colorful beaded friendship bracelets for their new friends to remember them by. Diona handed them a little card that explained what each color represented. Athens, Abigail, Natalie, and Addison thanked them for their hospitality and gifts, then went on their way but ended up getting lost, and found themselves by the black hole. They quickly decided to turn around and go the other way when a dark shadow pushed Abigail, causing her to stumble. She toppled into Athens, knocking him off the face of the Earth into the large black hole. She covered her eyes as guilt ripped through her heart, not wanting to look down, though Athens wasn't gone yet. He struggled to hang on. His fingers were bleeding as he gripped onto the rock's edge. Addison looked down and saw him.

Without thinking, he grabbed ahold of his hand. Their hearts pounded as the adrenaline rushed through their bodies all at once. Using every ounce of energy he had, Addison pulled Athens out of the black hole. Falling backward, they hit the freezing cold ground.

"I'm not sure I could have ever forgiven myself if anything had happened to you. Thank God for putting that ledge near the edge." Abigail grabbed Athens' arm and hugged him. "Let's get out of here. This is one place I'd like to forget." Addison said as he got up from the icy cold ground.

"No doubt. The sooner we leave, the better." Athens shook off the snow then remembered a small lighthouse they'd passed along the way. Natalie perched herself on Athens' shoulder while heading back to the secret rock.

The trio of friends locked arms and stood back-to-back. Then Athens whispered, "Guide me in Your truth and teach me Your ways, oh Lord, for You are my God, my Savior, my hope is in You all day long." Instantly, they disappeared into the United States, wearing American clothing, ready and united to take on whatever comes their way.

Fun Facts:

- Wolf Blood Moon's and glow worms are super rare.

- Stones of Eilat are only found in King Solomon's Mine in Israel and can be purchased online.

- Deception Island is in Antarctica. The black hole really exists and keeps growing bigger; it keeps appearing and disappearing. It's believed that Nephillim use the black hole to travel through.

- The story about the secret remnant of Athens' hair is made up from Ezekiel 5:1-5 found in the Bible.

- The Crucifix catfish, also known as the Sail Catfish, is super cool. Athens has the one in the picture.

- The Aurora Borealis lights in Alaska are magnificent.

- <u>Look on page 172 to learn more about salvation.</u>

CHAPTER 6

A MYSTERIOUS PHENOMENON

THE SWORD OF THE SPIRIT

Yosemite National Park, California

"Wow," was the first word Athens spoke when he stepped off the rock into America. Abigail's head was still spinning, and Addison stood with a stunned look on his face.

Eliza twirled into the atmosphere like a beaming starlight. "I see you've gained another piece of the armor."

"Yes, each piece is truly magnificent, and their powers are remarkable. I feel more confident with each step I take toward my destiny. I know the battle is far from over, but my vision of meeting the King grows stronger every day." Athens looked out at the surrounding scenery as they stood at the base of a giant waterfall and watched as the sun was setting. Eliza gestured at the

116

beautiful falls. "Deep in the forest are many of God's wondrous creations. There's a natural phenomenon that seamlessly occurs in the midst of the woods between the treetops and the mountain peaks leading into the valley below. You can see wondrous waterfalls flowing down into magical places with hundreds of acres of wildlife and living things." Eliza said as she placed her hand next to her ear to listen. "Bridal Veil Falls is a treasured spot, noted for its grandeur, ageless beauty. By day, you can hear the sweet melodies of chirping birds, humming insects, and nature's wondrous sounds. By night, it's called Yosemite Firefall. You can see the illumination of thousands of flashes and flares with brilliant lights shooting across the sky as the forest comes to life. Only those fortunate enough to come here during the right time of year will ever get to experience its natural phenomenon."

"What do you mean? Are we here at the right time of year?" Natalie twittered.

"You'll just have to wait and see. People travel near and far to experience its rushing red river that appears like glowing lava that flows three thousand feet downslope into a valley of streams. This natural phenomenon is created when the cold mountain air meets the last rays of sunlight just after sunset. During the moonbeam hour, waves of light seep down from heaven and shoot across the sky at just the right speed at just the right angle at just the right time. This magnificent phenomenon is faithful to appear every year." Eliza said. Then her voice dropped to a whisper. "There's something else you should know. Long ago, in this old forest, there were once giant creatures. These weren't any ordinary giants.

"Everyone greatly feared them." They could uproot trees and move stones weighing over a thousand pounds each. If you listen closely, you might even hear the echoing sounds of the slumbering, snoring giants who laid sleeping beneath the tall sequoia trees of long ago. These giants were not friendly at all but were horrible and wicked creatures. Their sole existence was to capture humans who passed through the valley of a forgotten time. The giants stole children from their families in the night, and offered them up to their gods as human sacrifices, during the bewitching hour, by throwing them into an open fire. Once the bones became red-hot embers, they poured them over the waterfall to their idol gods, imitating the glowing, red river to mock the natural beauty that God had created."

Athens and his friends didn't like the sound of that story at all. Athens' eyes peered off into the forest as Eliza had left. Then they decided to build a fire, so they collected sticks build a fire. Next they gathered piles of leaves to sleep on before huddling up for the night, while hoping to forget about the monstrous giants in their heads.

"Let's sing a song. I'll lead the harmony," Abigail suggested when a little glimmer of light showed up beside them. It was a tiny, friendly firefly. This wasn't an ordinary firefly at all. He had noble-like qualities and could light the night for others to see.

"Who are you?" Athens asked, knowing, of course, he was in an enchanted forest where anything was possible.

"My name is Zeek, short for Ezekiel. I'm a lightning bug, and I'm here to help. I'm a guardian of the forest. I carry the light of hope with me. The forest can be extremely dangerous with wild beasts and creatures that lurk in the shadows. You'll be safer with the light. Would you like me to bring you more?"

"Yes please, that would be great, but wait, I thought you were a firefly," Athens replied.

"We are one and the same. We are glowing insects that glimmer and shine in the dark. People call us by different names, but I choose to be called Zeek, the lightning bug. Even the God of the universe has many names. Some call Him Yahweh, Yeshua, El Shadai, Elohim, or God Almighty. He answers to all of those," Zeek explained.

An old owl hooted in a nearby tree. Abigail shuddered. "It's a little scary out here. We sure could use Him out here right about now." She said.

"My family can keep you warm and safe throughout the night." Zeek said, as he saw a spark of hope ignite in their eyes after promising to return with his family. "I'll be back." Zeek said as he took flight into the night air.

Addison and Natalie gathered more sticks and twigs then tossed them into the fire pit. Athens and Abigail moved closer to the fire and rubbed their hands together.

Crackling and popping noises arose from the flames that released sparks and embers into the atmosphere. Images began to surface. At first, they weren't sure what to make of it, then the face of a roaring lion appeared, along with a raging bear, and a grand eagle who flew above the flames. The images looked so surreal, as if the animals were telling their own stories. Athens and his friends were mesmerized as they gazed into the sparks of fire. Without warning, a seven-headed, ten-horned dragon

formed out of the bottom of the burning pit! It seemed to be staring them right in their faces. Tingles shot up and down Athens' spine. It looked like the dragon from his dream. "Please don't come to life, please don't come to life," Abigail whispered. Addison scooted away from the fire. Then the image of the dragon vanished in the flames. Athens wondered what this had to do with him. He wanted to start searching for the last piece of armor, but he wouldn't likely find it in the dark. He couldn't see the whole picture of what was yet to come, but he could sense something lurking in the dark. Athens pulled out his globe and gazed into it, hoping to get another glimpse of heaven to comfort his heart. He spun it around and around, viewing all seven continents, stopping at Israel to envision what the great city of Jerusalem would look like. The streets were made of solid gold. A vision of the King's mansion garden appeared in the spotlight.

It was getting late, and the campfire turned cold. Shadows drew near as they quietly watched and waited. "Where's Zeek?" Abigail asked. They hung their heads in disappointment. Nearly giving up all hope, Athens' heavy eyelids drooped. He almost closed them completely when off in the distance, the trees began flickering with lights. A multitude of lightning bugs came beaming over the hills into the campsite, with Zeek leading the way. A trail of lights danced beneath the moonlight. The lightning bugs created amusing patterns and designs. Some formed lanterns in the trees, while others created a halo around Athens' head. He looked like a royal prince. More of them made a crown over Abigail's head. She looked like a princess. They gave Addison wings, so he appeared to be an angel from heaven. Athens laughed.

"What a creative, bright family you have, Zeek. They're very talented," Abigail remarked.

Zeek's light grew brighter. "Is there anything else we can do for you while we're here?" Athens thought for a moment before responding. "Well, actually, yes. We're in search of a sword called the Sword of the Spirit. Have you ever heard of it?"

"The sword you speak of is not just an ordinary sword wielded by human hands. It was forged in the heavenly realms. It can give life and take it away. It's sharper than any two-edged sword and has equal power both in the physical and spiritual world. It's on the other side of the valley beneath the crystal waterfalls, but not just anyone can remove it. The hand of God placed it there, and only the hand of God can remove it," Zeek replied.

"I understand," said Athens. "I've been sent here to find it and to prove myself worthy. King Elohim has invited me into His kingdom. If I stay true to the task and finish this quest before midnight tomorrow, my friends and I will receive a great inheritance. I must defeat the enemy and proclaim victory over darkness and the evil forces of the world."

"Let's pray and hope that you find what you're looking for," Zeek's light flickered.

"Lord of lords and King of kings, creator of all things, thank you for giving us more than we deserve and for loving us as much as You do. Please put a hedge of protection over Athens and his friends. Keep evil far from them. Give them wisdom, courage, and strength for the journey ahead. We trust all things will work together for the good of your people. In Jesus mighty name, Amen."

"Now, I know for sure. He will be with us through the night," Athens blinked his eyes. No sooner had he laid his head down to rest; he began to sink into a deep sleep. The lightning bugs made themselves at home, keeping watch over them throughout the night.

Athens was dreaming of a sweeter life, living in the land of milk and honey, with his family and friends when he realized he had a fear equal to his fear of heights. Suddenly, that fear came to life. He heard a tremendous noise and felt the earth shaking beneath his body. Giants roamed the area, stomping through the woods, uprooting the trees, and overturning boulders to find him. As soon as they laid eyes on him, he took off running in the opposite direction. The massive sequoia trees transformed into an incredible maze. Maybe they wouldn't find him in here, but without warning, one of them reached down, grabbed ahold of Athens with its giant fists, and plucked him from the ground. Athens was dangling upside down by his ankles. The giants were taking him to their altar to be sacrificed to their gods. Athens struggled to get away, but the giant's grip was too tight. He couldn't get loose, he tried yelling for help, kicking, and screaming, but no words came out of his mouth. *How could he escape?*

Again, he yelled for help, but nothing happened. He tried a third time, and still, no words were spoken. Panic seized his insides. The giant squeezed him tighter. He could barely breathe. But he would not give up hope. He was determined and yelled again. This time, he forced the air right out of his mouth in a loud, clear voice. "Jesus, help me!" The sound of his own voice woke him from his dreadful nightmare. His eyes were wide open, the palms of his hands were sweaty, and his heart was racing so fast that he could barely catch his breath. He looked around to see where he was and realized he was still in the forest lying on a bed of leaves, but all the lightning bugs were gone. He was alone. *It was nearly morning, but where did everybody go?* A rustling sound came from the branches and leaves in the trees. It was getting closer.

"Oh, no." He quickly jumped to his feet and grabbed his backpack as he prepared to run. *Was it giants coming after him through the trees?* He started moving for fear of getting eaten alive when out of the bushes appeared Abigail and Addison. "Thank God, it's only you. You scared me. I just had the worst nightmare ever." His heart nearly skipped a beat. "What were you two doing anyway?"

"We found some snacks for breakfast," Abigail said delightedly.

"What is it?" Athens asked. "Seeds from a sequoia tree and figs from a fig tree. They're quite tasty." She said.

"I'd love to try some, too." Natalie chirped. She hopped on one foot and grasped some seeds with the other.

"Just think, tomorrow night, we could be feasting with King Elohim," Abigail said while eating her figs and seeds.

"I can only imagine how wonderful the food will be," Addison said as he handed Athens some figs.

"All you can eat for sure, feasting for seven years, I can't wait!" Athens said while taking a bite of his fig.

"By the way, what was your dream about?"

Abigail asked as she handed him some seeds.

"I dreamed there were giants in the forest, and they captured me and wanted to sacrifice me to their gods."

"Thank God it was only a dream." Natalie peeped.

Addison's eyes got big. "Yes, but it could be a warning."

"We have to be super careful. We are so close to the end of our journey. We can't let anything stop us," Athens said as he moved closer to Abigail to get more seeds.

"We can bring what we don't eat with us on our journey to share with the people in the Promised Land," Abigail suggested.

"Great idea, but I have to admit I'm pretty hungry. I'm not sure those seeds and figs are enough to hold me over," Addison chuckled.

"No worries, we will find more food somewhere else when we get to Israel, have a little faith." Athens grinned.

They began searching for the sword when the trees began swaying back and forth. The branches were bent halfway back and became separated by the wind giving them a view behind the trees. Behold, an eclipse of gorgeous, white moths gathered together and formed a life-sized sword, pointing north. Abigail's lips parted. "I think we should follow them." Athens stretched out his arms, and one landed in the palms of his hands. Abigail and Natalie were trying to catch one. "Don't try so hard. Let them come to you," he suggested.

Like a streak of light, Eliza appeared. "These moths are special." She said as one landed on her finger.

She pointed out the black markings on their wings. "If you look closely one way, you can see a sword and a shield, but when you turn them around the other way, you can see a cross and a shield."

"They're breathtaking! What are they called?" Abigail asked as one fluttered into her hands. Natalie was trying her best to catch one.

"The moths are called Jesus moths because of their unique markings." She remarked.

"Very impressive. They remind me of the Sword of the Spirit," Athens suggested as he looked at it closely.

"The sword works best when the word of God is spoken from our hearts. And the Spirit of God becomes present in our lives, working in us and moving through us and is sharper than any two-edged sword."

"God creates the most incredible things!" Abigail said. "The word of God breathes life into the believer and gives hope and strength so that no weapon can form against them or you," Eliza explained.

"Yes, that's it, you're right!" Athens said. "Everything is perfectly clear. If you look closely enough, you can find Jesus in most everything." His words can cast out all fear and doubt too." A kaleidoscope of moths flew up from behind the bushes, all having the faces of Jesus on the backs of their wings. "How marvelous," Abigail gasped.

"Listen," Athens heard a faint howling noise. "Shhh, it sounded like wolves." Natalie spread her wings and flew to the treetops to have a look around. She returned scared and couldn't speak.

Addison reached for a branch and climbed up a tree to see if he could spot what frightened her. From a distance, a large dark wolf-like creature lumbered within the forest. It had two terrifying heads with four sets of sharp devilish eyes both in front and the back of its head. It was followed by a pack of wolves. Addison climbed back down the tree and described what he had seen. Natalie shivered. "We can't let them find us. Let's head to the river and swim downstream. It's just beyond that circle of trees." Addison said.

"They're coming for you. You must hide," Eliza motioned for them to hurry. She created an invisible barrier between them. They fled to the riverbank, hoping nothing could follow their scent, but the river looked as if it was covered with sheets of shiny glass that sparkled like crystal. Downstream, there were twelve stepping-stones to lead them across the water. Athens stared into the icy glass river, thinking about what was up ahead. Then, he squeezed his eyes shut for just a second, then opened them. "We need to Trust God to protect us."

"Let's do it!" Addison said, moving forward.

"I'll go first." Abigail jumped across the stones and lost her balance, plunging into the icy cold river. The current pulled her downstream. Athens had no choice but to go in after her. He dove in and swam as fast as he could. A long piece of driftwood floated a few feet away. Swimming against the current, he grabbed ahold of it then kicked his feet, propelling him over to help her. Abigail's head bobbed up and down in the cold water. Athens yelled, "rise above it, rise above it. Don't let it sink you, don't let it sink you!" He finally made it over to her and quickly grabbed her hand as she reached for the driftwood, then he wrapped his arm around her. They were slowly moving forward, trying to keep their heads above water while kicking their feet against the strong current until it picked up speed and pushed them faster downstream. Their faith and hope kept them afloat.

A raging vortex formed in the water, swirling in circles, sucking everything up in its path, causing sheets of ice to break away from the riverbank. Like icy daggers they moved downstream after them. Athens and Abigail were being pulled into the emerging vortex.

Athens tried to figure out a way to get out of the dangerous, cold merging waters when he saw an old broken-down bridge up ahead. Holding on with one arm around the driftwood and one arm for paddling, he prepared their escape. Abigail continued kicking her legs against the current while clinging on for dear life. "Hold on tight Abigail, we're going to crash!"

The driftwood plowed directly into the bridge and teetered back and forth between two pieces of timber before it came to a jolting stop. The strong current pulled Athens away from the bridge. Exhaustion was setting in, and his hope of escaping was fading. Not giving up, he managed to grab ahold of one of the posts and pull himself to safety. "Abigail, let go of the driftwood." She reached for Athen while trying to pull herself out of the water and lunged onto his back and climbed out. Addison and Eliza followed along the riverbank and leaped across the twelve stones to make their way to the other side of the river. Natalie flew ahead to meet them. Athens and Abigail laid on the riverbank to catch their breath. Minutes later, Addison and Eliza caught up to them.

"I'm so glad you guys are okay," Addison said as he knelt beside them. "That vortex was petrifying. I think it's gonna be a miracle if we make it to Israel in one piece."

Athens raised his head to speak but instead pointed to a sparkling waterfall of enormous size and splendor that was just beyond the riverbank. There were rocks piled on top of rocks as far as the eye could see, leading to the top of a mountain range that created a magical vista.

The Sword of the Spirit glistened and sparkled in the crystal clear pool of water near the bottom of the waterfall as it reflected from the sun's light.

Athens stood on shaky legs and gaped in awe for a moment. Then he walked over to the sword. Out of thin air, the hands of God formed and separated the crystal, clear waters into two. Athens stepped into the dry, rocky area at the bottom of the pool. The cool, flowing waters splashed his face as he reached for the sword. Like magic, the stream of living water poured out over him. Completely covering him from head to toe. The anointing power of God filled his heart and mind. Goosebumps covered his entire body as he graciously accepted the sword. His friends stared in awe as they witnessed the outpouring of the Holy Spirit baptizing him. Then the hands of God slowly began to dissolve and vanished right before their eyes. Athens proudly carried the sword out of the water as his chest rose and fell. He felt empowered as he led his friends back to the hidden rock. "This is the last time we'll be linking arms together. Our quest is nearly over." Athens said.

"It's hard to believe, but man, I can't wait to get to Israel," Addison said enthusiastically.

"All for one and one for all," Abigail raised her hands in the air and shouted.

Without delay, the words seemed to float off his lips. "Guide me in Your Truth and teach me Your ways, oh Lord, for You are my God, my Savior, my hope is in You all day long!" In the twinkling of an eye, a strong breeze wrapped around them and took them away.

Fun Facts:

- ⸲ Many languages are spoken in America because people travel from all over the world to live here. It's the home of the free and the brave. In God we trust is written on all the currency.

- ⸲ The majestic sequoia redwood trees in California are the largest in the world and live longer than most. They can reach 367 feet tall and 22 feet wide and can produce 400,000 seeds per tree every year.

- ⸲ The natural phenomenon at Bridal Veil Falls, California, occurs every year for two weeks at the end of February.

- ⸲ Two types of Jesus moths exist in America. You may even spot one by accident.

- ⸲ Jesus was baptized by John the Baptist in the Jordan River. God desires for us to be baptized by water once we become believers. Take a step of faith and follow Him. Athens is in the picture on the right, being baptized by Pastor Kelly from our church.

- ⸲ <u>The armor pieces are spiritual weapons Christians use to defeat spiritual enemies. See page 174.</u>

Chapter 7

THE KINGS MANSION

THE FINAL DESTINATION

Jerusalem, Israël

Filled with excitement, Athens and his friends were out of breath when they stepped through the portal after entering Israel. They were wearing robust yet simple garments to keep them cool. Athens' sandals were firmly fitted on his feet, with the Belt of Truth secured around his waist. Abigail wore a beautiful dark blue scarf wrapped around her head called a hijab. She felt the soft silk between her fingers as she admired it.

"You look pretty, Abigail. You'll fit right in for sure," Addison said, smiling.

"Thank you. She said smiling back, you never know who you might meet. I wonder when Eliza will be joining us?"

Athens was dying to meet the King face to face as he wiped the sweat from his brow. He wished he could rest for a moment underneath a nice shady tree. Exhausted and thirsty, he felt as if they'd never make it to the King's mansion in time. Yet it was the hope in his heart that kept him moving.

Addison and Natalie looked around but didn't see much beyond the hot sandy dunes while Athens and Abigail dropped to their knees in the sand with the scorching sun on their heads. Athens glanced over at Abigail and cracked a smile, but Abigail looked as though she was going to pass out. Her cheeks were flush, her lips were chapped, and her tongue was so dry she could hardly speak. Abigail turned away for a moment and rubbed her temples while staring off into the distance. "I'm starting to miss home, aren't you?" she asked.

"Yeah, I miss home, too." Athens lifted his eyes to heaven and began to pray, asking Jesus to bring him a shade of hope. In an instant, a strong breeze passed by. The debris on the ground moved in an upward spiraling, motion twirling next to them. It moved faster and faster until a Palm tree sprang forth from it. The Palm tree was large enough for the two of them to sit beneath to cool off. And not a minute too soon. Athens slumped over in the sand, and Abigail nearly fainted against the bottom of the tree trunk.

Addison walked over to stand beneath the tree when a coconut fell from the treetop and cracked open after hitting him smack on the head. "Ouch, what was that?" He yelled while rubbing his sore sticky wet head. "Am I bleeding?" He looked down at his hands expecting to see blood but it was only milk.

"Are you okay?" Abigail asked while trying not to laugh. "Coconut milk, my favorite. Is there any left for me?" She reached for the coconut and broke it all the way open.

"I'll have some too, please," Natalie peeped.

"What a perfect tree," Athens said as Abigail panted beneath it.

"Yep, it is," she responded, looking up at the tree. "God is so good."

"Yes, He is. I totally get it now." Addison looked up while rubbing the bump on his head.

"We're sorry for snickering, but it looked so funny when the coconut landed on your head," Abigail still giggling.

"No problem, I'm fine," he said as he wiped the milk off his hands.

Breathing a sigh of relief, Athens mustered up the energy to stand on his feet. They were getting ready to start walking when they could hardly believe their eyes. A man with three donkeys walked toward them.

"These are very special donkeys that will take you where you need to go," he said.

"Thank you, that's very kind of you." Athens approached one of the donkeys and stroked its back. The donkeys have the shape of a cross woven into the fur on their backs. *What did this mean?* Athens was about to ask, but the man disappeared without a trace. *"It must be a gift from God,"* Athens looked to the north and then to the south. But he didn't see anything. His chest rose and fell.

"It's just what we need to take us into town," Abigail added.

Like a flash of light, Eliza appeared, waving her hands above her head, trying to get their attention to show them the way to Bethlehem.

But, when she saw the donkeys, she immediately bowed and said, "Shalom." She straightened her back like a teacher and turned her attention to the three of them. "According to history, these donkeys are just like the one that Jesus rode into Jerusalem. This is how the donkeys inherited the name Jerusalem donkey. Long ago, everyone stood in the streets, watching and waving their palm branches in the air to celebrate their King, who they called the Messiah. People placed their coats on the ground along with palm branches for the King to ride across. After all, He was an extraordinary King, and they wanted to give Him the royal treatment."

"Kind of like rolling out the red carpet to honor someone for something they did in today's society," said Abigail.

"Your exactly right. Everyone shouted, Hosanna, Hosanna, praising the King of the Jews, as He rode into town on His donkey. Every year, right before Easter, many people around the world celebrate this incredible event called Palm Sunday. Legend has it that the donkey loved his master so much that he couldn't bear to leave Him when He died on the cross. So, as the sun was setting, it cast a shadow on the donkey's back, forever marking him with the symbol of the cross to remind us of the donkey's love and devotion for his King."

Eliza walked over and rubbed the neck of one of the donkeys. "The Jerusalem donkeys were, in fact, sent here by God and will carry you into the town of Bethlehem, where you can find a place to stop for food and water before heading into the Old City of Jerusalem."

"Let's get going," Athens snapped his fingers like a prince as he climbed onto the donkey's back.

"Why are we going to Bethlehem first?" Abigail asked.

"To visit the town where Jesus was born, of course," Eliza replied.

Abigail tried to climb on her donkey but fell to one side and landed on her head with her arms and legs dangling beside her—a silly, awkward position. Athens laughed.

The donkey turned around to see what was going on as she made another attempt. This time she flipped around and ended up facing the donkey's rear end. Her belly was pressed across the donkey's back, with her arms propped up and her legs crisscrossed behind her head, sticking up in the air. She looked like she had horns growing out the back of her head. She sighed. "Ugh! This is harder than it looks." She was still facing the wrong way, and the donkey's butt couldn't be any fun to look at.

Athens and Addison were laughing so hard they couldn't stop. Natalie tweeted and encouraged her to try again. Abigail gave it one last try. Leaping higher than before, she finally turned around, got it right, and grabbed hold of the reins. "That a girl, are you comfy now?" Athens asked.

She glared at him and lifted her chin. "Well, I've never done this before, and quite honestly, I never want to do it again. I'm totally exhausted," Abigail murmured under her breath. "Note to self; never ride on another animal's back, ever again." With a pull of the reins, they were off and running.

A short distance ahead, they saw a man pushing a large cart who appeared to be carrying over one hundred loaves of bread.

"Where do you suppose he's going with all that bread?" Abigail asked.

"Probably to the marketplace in Bethlehem," Athens said.

As soon as they entered the city, they met a woman filling her water vessel. She smiled as Athens passed by. "Are you here to meet the King?"

"Which king are you referring to?" he asked.

She lowered her head and whispered in his ear, "Well, the King of kings, of course."

"Yes, how did you know?" Athens waited for her to answer. He looked up into the sky and saw a white dove passing over their heads.

"A little bird told me," she answered. "Our thirst for water is essential. It's like bees are to honey or a king to his kingdom. Without a purpose, life is meaningless." She bowed her head and softly said. "Shalom, peace be with you."

Athens smiled and said. "Shalom."
He noticed her water vessel was still sitting on the ledge full of water. "Wait."

He dashed over and picked it up, but when he turned around, she was already gone. "Another mystery," he whispered.

The man carrying the loaves of bread passed through an archway covered with grapevines. The sweet delicate fruit dangled from above their heads.

They watched the man park his cart near a two-story building surrounded by beautiful Palm trees. They could almost taste the freshness of the bread as the aroma lingered beneath their noses. When the man turned and walked toward the local eateries, Athens noticed writing on the back of his shirt. He squinted his eyes to read it. *Bethlehem, The House of Bread.* "Interesting, I didn't know that Bethlehem means ~ House of Bread?" He said.

"I'd sure like to have some right now," Addison replied.

A young woman was sitting at a table, cradling her newborn baby. She gently stroked his cheek and sang him a lullaby as she waited to be served. Athens continued to look around and observed twelve men waiting to be seated inside.

"Who do you think those men are?" Addison asked.

"I don't know, but let's see if we can join them," Athens had a gut feeling that he was supposed to meet them.

"No, no," Abigail replied. "I don't want to be bothered. I mean, I don't want to bother them. Why don't you guys go ahead? I'll go take care of the donkeys in the stables."

"Okay, we'll see you later then," said Athens and off they went. When Athens and Addison entered the room, a strong breeze blew in as if the Holy Spirit of God entered the room with them. All eyes turned toward them. Athens felt led to walk over to the men when one of them invited him to join their group in the upper room.

These were not just any ordinary men but men of great importance, men of peace and honor. They were, in fact, called Disciples, who were men of God and followers of Jesus. Athens was glad to be a guest at their table and introduced himself first.

A golden menorah light was placed in the center of each of the long white wooden tables, along with a bowl of fresh fruit, a warm basket of bread, a cool pitcher of water, and one chalice. As they sat down, one of the men picked up the breadbasket and passed it around the table for everyone to share. He told them not to eat the bread until everyone held a piece in their hand. Next, he filled the chalice with the fruit of the vine.

"Everyone, now raise your bread and give thanks to God for all your blessings, praising the name of Yeshua—the King of kings and Lord of lords, for all that He's done, for all that He's doing and for all that is yet to come. The bread represents the body of Jesus, and the wine represents the blood of Jesus. He is the greatest King ever born. He has the power to give life and to take it away. He's a True Promise Keeper. He's the light in the darkness. Jesus said to break the bread and eat it and to take the fruit of the vine and drink the wine, in remembrance of Him."

"This is called communion," Simon said. "Jesus is the bread of life." Everyone nodded to agree as they ate their bread and drank the wine from the chalice.

One of the disciples, named Judas, got up to leave the table and stopped to ask Athens how much he would be willing to sell his donkey for, but Athens told him the donkey was not for sale.

"Surely, you must have a price?" he asked.

Again, Athens replied. "No, I'm sorry, he's not for sale. I need him to take me to the Mount of Olives in Jerusalem."

"I'll pay you a great sum of money for him," Judas suggested for a third time as he tried to give Athens a bag of silver, but Athens told him no. "What's so special about your donkey anyway?" he asked.

One of the men, named Matthew, got up and looked out the window. He noticed the crosses on the donkey's backs, "now I know why you don't want to sell him. He's a very special donkey that came from the great city of Jerusalem." Athens walked over and peered out the window.

Simon walked across the room to speak to Athens. "Did you know that Jesus was called the King of the Jews? Not long after that, the people turned their backs on Him and betrayed Him. He was falsely accused and beaten. Then He was led to His death on the cross during the Jewish feast of Passover. The people of Israel use to sacrifice lambs for their sins until Jesus came and died on the cross. He became the last living sacrifice given for the sins of the world. He was buried in a rich man's tomb and rose from the grave after the third day." Athens was staring out of the window.

Another disciple chimed in to speak. "Witnesses saw Jesus for forty days before he ascended into heaven. He empowered His disciples, giving them spiritual gifts from the Holy Spirit to carry out His work throughout Israel and all the world. Jesus performed great miracles, like feeding multitudes of people when there wasn't enough food to eat." Simon handed Addison the breadbasket and said, "Jesus healed the sick and gave sight to the blind. He gave up His earthly life for us all so that we could have eternal life with Him." Just then Natalie flew in and picked up some bread crumbs off the floor and ate them.

Simon turned to his friends with a smile and said, "one day, all people—men, women, and children of every nation, color, and tongue—will stand before the judgment seat of God. Everyone will be held accountable for their actions. God will give many rewards and punishments on that great day." Addison crossed his arms and placed his hand under his chin to think.

"Do you know that God has many names?" Asked John, who was another disciple. "The name *Messiah* in Hebrew means Anointed One. *King Elohim* means the Living God, the One True God, and *Yeshua* is the Hebrew name that means Jesus!"

***

Abigail entered the stables carrying some treats for the donkeys to eat when she heard one of the donkeys talking. Abigail's mouth dropped open, and her food slipped out.

"I had no idea you could talk too," she said.

"We only speak when we have something to say; like when you tried climbing on my back, all we wanted to do was laugh." The donkeys all started laughing. "Hee-haw, hee-haw, hee-haw!"

"Yeah, that was quite entertaining." Abigail shook her head and just looked at them with her hands on her hips. "Seriously! You try climbing on the back of something with four legs that is twice your size and see how that works out for you because it's definitely not easy!"

"Yeah, we could tell, but it sure looked like a lot of fun," said one of the other donkeys as they continued laughing. "Hee-haw, hee-haw, hee-haw. This is one day I won't forget." Said one of the donkeys.

"Some thanks I get for taking care of you." She crossed her arms. "I think I'll go see what the guys are doing."

***

A while later, Simon invited them to his house for dinner. They kindly accepted and were honored to be his guest. Addison picked up another piece of bread and ate it before leaving. Athens and his friends including the three donkeys followed Simon home. Athens realized meeting Simon was no coincidence but, in fact, another divine appointment. God put them in the right place at just the right time on just the right day.

Simon's home was a small, modest house that was nicely decorated and had a pleasant scent to it. The smell of incense filled the air. "Make yourself at home. Feel free to go wash up before dinner," Simon said as he pointed down the hall to the washroom. There were clean white linens hanging in the bathroom and freshly cut flowers placed in the center of the kitchen table.

Athens noticed a garden in his backyard filled with lovely fruits and vegetables. His stomach growled. He could hardly wait to eat dinner because he didn't eat much after taking communion at the restaurant.

With a knock on the door, Simon welcomed eight more friends into his home. Two of the ladies were sisters named Mary and Martha. Athens was inspired by Mary's devotion to God and enjoyed her company as they sat around the table and shared stories.

While enjoying some stuffed grape leaves, pita bread, olives and cheese for dinner Athens explained that his journey had shown him the depths of God's power, love, and mercy. It helped him to understand and recognize who he is and who Jesus is. Jesus is the Son of God and man. He is the same yesterday, today, and forever. He still performs all sorts of miracles every day and has gone to prepare a mansion for us in HIS KINGDOM.

After dinner, Simon and his friends took out their wood wind instruments and played wonderful music while the others joined in to sing a new song of praise, giving glory to the King of Kings. When it was time to go, Athens, Abigail and Addison thanked them for their hospitality and embraced their new friends with warm hugs and handshakes.

"Friends for life," Athens said smiling.

"Shalom ~ Peace be with you," Simon said as they parted ways. Traveling onward, Athens and his friends approached the valley near the Mount of Olives. Completely mesmerized, they stood in awe for a moment to soak it all in. Never in a million years could they have imagined a place with such beautiful rolling hills, hundreds upon hundreds of Royal Palm trees and luscious rows of Olive trees. It left them speechless.

Upon entering Jerusalem, the Great City of Old, two men dressed in white sackcloth were standing on the roadside. One was preaching on how to get to heaven, and the other was sounding his shofar horn, making a great noise, shouting in the streets telling people to repent and turn away from their sins. Athens cracked a smile. Surely, they must know King Elohim. The two men glanced his way while squinting their eyes as they appeared to be looking right through him. They nodded their heads and acknowledged Athens as he approached.

Immediately he stopped to speak with the two men. These were not ordinary men but were men sent by God. One of them opened his mouth and flames of fire blew out of it. "Behold, there's a great danger that lies ahead of you. Beware of the prince of the air, Lucifer, that great and dreadful beast, the red dragon having seven heads and ten horns plans to crush and destroy you."
A lump formed in Athens' throat. Meeting the two men was no accident but a divine appointment to give him words of wisdom and fair warning.

Before anyone realized it, an angry mob approached from behind and started throwing sticks and stones at them. The two prophets told the mob to stop it and to turn away from their sins before it was too late.

The prophets came to share a message of truth and had hoped to lead the people to Jesus for salvation. "The only way to get to heaven is to repent and ask Jesus to come into your life." One of the prophets said.

"He is the Bread of Life. No one can enter the Kingdom and receive the gift of Eternal Life except through Him." It was a simple message of hope to bring peace and love into the hearts and lives of anyone who wanted to listen, but most of the people's hearts were already hardened.

"What if we don't want eternal life?" someone shouted.

"Yeah, what if we don't want to live forever?"
Another one said.

Athens frowned. "There are only two choices, Heaven or Hell. You should take your pick and choose wisely before it's too late."

God's prophets told the people what would happen to them if they didn't stop doing bad things and stop chasing after their idols, but they didn't listen because they no longer cared about what was right or wrong. They did what they wanted, when they wanted, without care. But Athens was sad for them. This could be their last chance to hear the truth and prepare their hearts to meet the King of kings, knowing that the day of judgment was coming soon.

One of the prophets held up his hands and spoke, "Your left hand is your past, your right hand is your future, and you are standing in the middle. What will you do? Will you choose the right path and look to the future, or will you look to your past and keep on sinning?"

Not wanting to listen anymore, the mob tried to stop them from speaking and wanted to kill the two men of God, along with Athens and his friends.

One of the messengers blew flames of fire from his mouth, and injured some of the mob who continued to throw stones at them. Athens drew out his sword and shield. A shadow grew over their heads as the sky turned dark. Then a thick purple mist covered the land creating a mystical fog. Athens covered his head with his shield.

"What's happening? I can't see a thing in this fog,"Abigail cried as she motioned her hands back and forth, trying to see through the fog.

"Is this a good thing or a bad thing?" Addison bellowed.

"I don't know, is it toxic?" Abigail asked. They covered their noses and mouths with their clothes trying not to breathe the air.

Eliza appeared as a flash of light, urging Athens and his friends to run toward the old fortress that had a secret entrance near one of the cities gates. A sequence of seven angels gathered in the sky, each carrying a bowl of wrath. They carefully watched and waited for Athens and his friends to get to safety.

Through the dark purple, hazy fog came a surprise attack. Lucifer—the red dragon having seven heads and ten horns swooped down with his crooked tail and swiped away a third of the people. The creature then attacked the two messengers, killing them on the spot, leaving their bodies in the street for all to see. The evil people who were left behind rejoiced with gladness over their deaths. Some even exchanged gifts.

A loud horn sounded from the layers of clouds as they parted. Then a tremendous voice that could only be from God roared out of heaven, saying, *Come up here!*"

The messengers' dead bodies rose from the street and came back to life. They stood upon their feet and floated into the air. The mob trembled in fear with their mouths hanging open, as they watched the two men being taken up into heaven. The people were panicking, clearly afraid of what was going to happen to them.

The voice of God called out, saying to the seven angels dressed in white, *"Go and pour out your wrath."*

Each angel carried a different bowl of wrath, equaling seven in all. The angels released a punishment onto the people for what they had done—instantly killing three thousand of them. A third of them screamed and cried out in agony as boils and sores appeared on their skin. Locusts swarmed through the city, searching for crops to devour. Fires broke out everywhere. The people fell to their knees and lay on their faces, probably wishing for death, but death would not have them.

A foul scaly creature with deep dark glowing eyes crawled out of the sea like nothing anyone had ever seen before. The creature began marking all the people as the beast called them out by name, choosing them for his own. He marked them on the hand or their foreheads promising them all the world's riches, bringing peace and safety to the land. "Do you see the pain that God has put you through? I can protect you and give you the riches of the world if you follow me." The dragon declared.

No, no, no. The words sounded as sweet as honey, but the beast was lying.

Some of the people were tricked and took the mark on their hand or forehead, then the beast gathered them for his own. The dragon scooped them up with his giant talons and flew away. Their cries and screams echoed across the distance. A tear slipped down Athens' cheek as he heard their cries. It was too late. They could never escape the dragon's clutches now.

Before the dragon came back, Eliza took Athens and his friends safely underground into a hidden tunnel in the heart of Jerusalem. She called it Hezekiah's tunnel—a place where natural springs flowed into King David's old castle. Not far from the tunnel entrance, they discovered a secret storage room filled with armor, and charged weapons, including bows and arrows. Abigail and Addison chose their own weapons. Then crawled through the dark, damp tunnel before reaching the light at the end. They peered out and stood in a large courtyard near a long bridge that led to the other side of the city. Athens' heart picked up speed. *Could they be near the King's mansion?* Lucifer, the great red dragon, swooped down from the clouds as if he'd been tracking them all along. "Don't even think about it."

Lucifer bolted after Athens with his large, opened claws. Addison jumped in front of Abigail and pushed Athens out of the way. Holding tight to their weapons they drew back their bows and released silver-tipped arrows and spears, hoping to force him to retreat. The arrows burst on impact but did not stop the dragon. The great red dragon staggered to the ground, then shook it off and blew his fiery breath. He circled around and around, before regaining his strength. This time he aimed for Athens' head. Athens trembled with fear but wasn't about to let that stop him.

"Anyone who bears the mark of the beast will never enter heaven," the beast declared. The dragon snarled at him. Fury disfigured his many faces. But now, Athens was armed and ready. He had put on The Full Armor of God. The Helmet of Salvation was on his head with the Shield of Faith in front of him. The Belt of Truth was securely wrapped around his waist, and the Breastplate of Righteousness was in place to protect his heart. The Gospel Shoes of Peace were firmly fitted on his feet. He swiftly drew the Sword of the Spirit and stood his ground with his shield raised in the air, ready to block the fiery darts of the evil one.

Natalie spread her wings and took flight as she soared into the sky. Athens quickly realized what she was doing as she circled all seven of the dragon's ugly heads. She let out a piercing, screeching noise to distract the dragon. Addison and Abigail covered their ears. The dragon swooped down, stretching out all seven heads in Athens' direction. Athens swung around with a mighty blow and struck three of the dragon's heads all at once. The dragon plummeted down to the ground.

A multitude of angels watched from above. Abigail smiled and pointed to the sky. Everyone outside the city walls heard them cheering. "The great red dragon is slain," they shouted. "He's dead."

The angels blasted their trumpets. Then Athens looked up and turned his eyes toward the sunset as he stepped onto the bridge. His friends followed in his footsteps. The cherubim began signaling for the gate to open. King Elohim came forward to greet them at the east gate with open arms. Hundreds of soldiers stood at attention on the other side of the bridge. Without notice, that old evil dragon, having seven heads and ten horns, arose from his death and summoned his creatures from the abyss to join him. He wasn't done with Athens yet.

Athens took a firm stance and raised his hands above his head, aiming his sharp sword toward the red dragon.

153

Thunder and lightning fell from the sky, and shook the whole earth when a legion of angels bolted down from heaven on white horses. Their wings were covered with large eyes inside and out. Armed and ready for war, they were prepared to overthrow the demonic creatures and send them back to the abyss where they came from, but four more fearsome creatures appeared.

Each one had four heads with wings of steel and teeth like daggers. The look of death was in their eyes as they waged war against the angels.

Heavy winds blew in from the four corners of the earth, carrying angelic beings that were larger and more fierce than all the other angels put together. They soared through the air with their broad wings like that of great eagles and dispersed across the sky. Their heads were enormous like lions and their teeth were pearly white and as sharp as spears, their claws even more deadly. They surrounded the evil creatures. But the demonic creatures launched an attack and charged after Athens and his friends. Athens swiftly held up the Shield of Faith and a glowing golden aura of glory encircled him and his friends. The creatures were immediately burnt up when they hit the shield. There was nothing left of them but bone fragments, soot, and ashes. The smell of stench filled the air. It was awful.

A thousand lightning bolts violently struck the ground and opened up a large crack as deep as the Earth's core right outside the King's gate.

The angels threw the creatures down into the crevasse of the Earth as red-hot flames shot up from the ground.

The intense flames grew higher and hotter, oozing from what appeared to be a bottomless pit.

Without warning, a tremendous blazing fireball darted across the sky and struck the great red dragon.
It blinded the dragon's eyes and seared them shut, causing him to fall near the opening of the crevasse.

King Elohim gestured for Athens to throw the Sword of the Spirit into the heart of the dragon to rid the world of him once and for all. Athens advanced toward the dragon as adrenaline rushed through his veins. At the same time natural blue gases filled the atmosphere. He looked at the King, then looked at the dragon and launched the sword with all his might. Sparks of electricity rapidly flew from the sword and made their way directly into the dragon's heart, causing a huge explosion.

The dragon fell into the crevasse of the earth. It swallowed him up for all eternity. Blasts of trumpets blew louder and louder as shouts of triumph came from heaven above. At last, the sound of victory had been won. The golden harpists played an angelic tune. The cherubim sounded their horns once more. All the angels were singing and shouting from on-high as they descended from heaven, praising the King of kings. The dragon had been cast into the pit... Athens raised his hands in the air, praising God. "We did it."

Abigail ran toward him and wrapped her arms around him. "Oh my, I can't believe we really did it."

"Finally," Addison yelled as he chuckled, raising his fists into the air. "I've never seen anything like it in my life and I hope I never have to see it again."

King Elohim motioned for them to come near. Walking toward Him, they noticed seven golden lamp stands by each of the seven entrances leading to the mansion. The King met Athens and his friends at the garden gate.

"Please remove the armor and your shoes before entering. You no longer need them now that you're safely within the mansion walls. You only needed them to get you here." They took off their armor and placed it at the King's feet.

The King commanded one of His servants to bring forth a watering vessel from the well, along with three white robes. A crowd gathered around to watch.

"Athens, Abigail, and Addison, you are faithful and loyal Ambassadors." The King washed their feet, assuring them that it was necessary to wash away the dirt of the world before entering His Kingdom.

King Elohim brought forth *The Lamb's Book of Life.* "Inside this Golden Book are the names of those who are privileged to get to enter into my Kingdom. <u>The Golden Book reveals all the faithful, loyal servants and children of God.</u>" The book's cover had exquisite details of a beautiful hilltop with a lamb sitting beneath an olive tree, overlooking a sunrise. All four corners of the golden book had pictures of olive branches bearing fruit, giving evidence of how good life would be. The words Eternal Life were embossed on top of the book and lit up when the King ran His fingertips across them. He opened the cover, and all ears could hear the words being sung, *Holy, Holy, Holy is the Lamb of God. Holy is the King who does impossible things.*

Silver and gold sparks shot out of the book's pages like fireworks. A brilliant bright light covered each name as the King read them out loud. Athens' name and birthdate lit up first as it was announced.

From a prick of the King's finger, a drop of His blood marked the bottom of the page. He then used a stamp with three golden circles connected to three crowns on a three-headed lion to seal it, marking the date and time for all eternity. Athens leaned forward, staring at his birthdate. "Why is my birthday in the book, my King?"

"Since the beginning of time, My chosen prophets have kept close records of every generation. Every bloodline throughout the ages, including all the descendants of Jesus. Abraham, Isaac, and Jacob are also recorded in the scrolls. You are here with Me now because Jesus fulfilled every prophecy ever recorded about Him." The King kindly looked into Athens' eyes and continued. "Since you have accomplished your quest and have delivered all the armor pieces, there is only one thing left for Me to do."

The King stepped aside and the people moved over to reveal Athens' family and friends, who stood among the crowd of believers waiting to honor him. Athens' heart was bursting with great joy. Their smiles were upon him as he stood next to the King. "It's time to make you an heir to My Kingdom—a true prince. Wearing the armor gave you great strength, faith, and courage." The King looked upon Athens and his friends and smiled.

"Now, you'll never have anything to fear, doubt or worry about again. You have been chosen. I have adopted you and your friends as heir's into my Forever Kingdom."

Eliza handed King Elohim the most exquisite sword their eyes had ever seen. It must have been divinely crafted in the heavenly realms.

The King raised it over His head for everyone to see. The shine from the mirrored blade gave off a radiant glow from heaven as Athens stood before his King.

King Elohim told Athens to kneel so he got down on one knee and bowed his head. The mighty, powerful King tapped his right shoulder, then his left shoulder, and then tapped him on top of his head. "Now rise up a true, noble prince before your King." He said.

Looking at the tip of the shiny polished sword, Athens could see the depth and sharpness of the blade. The handle had an astonishing lion's head forged of gold with green emerald eyes and sparkling white teeth cut from diamonds. A chorus of heavenly voices rang out and rejoiced when Athens rose to his feet and became an heir to the King's throne. Eliza wore an innocent smile as she held the beautiful heirloom ring and golden crown of jewels for King Elohim.

The King took the ring and placed it on Athens' finger. Next, He placed the sparkling golden crown of jewels upon his head. "Thank you for allowing us to enter Your Kingdom," Athens said. Every knee was bent, every head was bowed, giving God great glory for all He has done! "I have crowned you with the jewels of victory over your enemies. You and your friends have proven yourselves to be trustworthy, faithful, and courageous. We have long prepared for this day." The King raised His hands above his head.

"You're all invited to our grand celebration and royal feast." He smiled and led everyone over to the grand ballroom. His arms were spread open wide. "Come, let the feast begin!" He exclaimed.

Athens leaned against a column and looked up into heaven through the open ceiling and saw the stars so numerous that he couldn't count them all. All their names had been written in *The Lamb's Book of Life* and would remain there forever. Every hand was clapping, and every voice was cheering as Abigail and Addison took their places in God's Kingdom next to Athens. And they all lived happily ever after!

Fun Facts:

- Jerusalem/Jesus donkeys are real animals with crosses on their backs. A talking donkey is mentioned in the Bible ~ Numbers 22:21-41. Read it and find out what happened.

- The purple mist really existed long ago near the Dead Sea in Israel and was very toxic.

- The meaning: four corners of the earth represent north, south, east, and west. Ancient scrolls exist and teach the lineage of Jesus going all the way back to the first man ever created, who was Adam.

- Christians take communion as a reminder to keep their promise to God by honoring His Son Jesus, who said to eat of the bread and drink of the wine in remembrance of Him. He covered our sins with His life and shed His blood on the cross for us. Before taking communion, we should always ask for forgiveness of our sins first, so we remain blameless and full of His love, honor, and grace.

- The two prophets are mentioned in the last book of the Bible in Revelation.

- The picture of the man carrying the loaves of bread is from Jerusalem.

- B.C. means before Christ & A.D. means Anno Domini ~ In the year of our Lord. Not after death, as many people believe. Time revolves around the birth of Jesus. Our birthday stems from the birth of Christ. From today's date, roughly 2021 years ago, is when He walked the Earth.

- God told the Israelites to put the blood of a lamb on their doorposts during Passover in the Old Testament. Now we know this symbolizes the blood of Jesus, who came into the world to be the last living sacrifice for all sin. Throughout **His**tory lambs were born in Bethlehem and then sacrificed in Jerusalem for the sins of people just like Jesus was.

- The great red dragon Lucifer, aka the devil, was mentioned in Revelation 12 in the Bible.

- Jesus' tomb in Israel became empty more than 2021 years ago.

- The year 2020 was known as the year of the locus. In the Bible, it talks about locus devouring everything in sight. Revelation 9:3.

- Dig deeper, look closer to uncover cool Bible stories in the book that you can discover on your own.

162

Become a Warrior for Jesus, and Serve!

- *Here are ways for you to help; Pray for us, our mission and God's vision.*

- *Volunteer in some fashion to help spread the word. Make flyers or advertise on social media.*

- *Give a donation to help support our ministry to get more books and programs into the hands of many people locally and worldwide.*

- *Soon to come will be a program designed to teach others how to suit up and put on the full Armor of God, while walking in peace and love, trusting in the name of Jesus!*

- *Contact me via email: Adventureswithathens1@gmail.com*

Belt of Truth

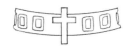

Ephesians 6:14
Stand firm then, with the belt of truth around your waist.

What is the belt of truth?
Who has the truth on their side?

The Belt of Truth is believing in God's word, to be the whole TRUTH through Jesus Christ. He's our reference point for right and wrong. The Bible was written to share the truth in its entirety. The Bible contains historical facts and records that have been proven over and over again. Not just part of it is true to suit our own needs, but all of it is true. Believers of Jesus Christ are Christians who trust and believe His word to be the truth, the Whole truth, and nothing but the truth. People who tell the truth about God's mighty word have the truth on their side.

John 14:6

Jesus said I am the way, the truth, and the life; no man comes to the Father except through me.

Psalms 25:5

Guide me in your truth and teach me, for you are God my Savior, and my hope is in you all day long.

Life Application:

We must always be truthful in all that we say and do so that we can walk upright, holding our heads up high, knowing we have the truth on our side. Presenting ourselves blameless before God. Lies cause us to have a guilty conscience and can hurt us and others around us in the long run. It affects our relationship we have with God and others. By telling the truth, we are righteous in Christ. Nothing can stand against the power of God Almighty.

John 3:18

He who trusts and believes in Him is Not judged, for there is no rejection, but he who doesn't believe is judged already because he has not trusted and believed in the trusted name of the only begotten son of God.

John 8:31

If you hold to my teachings, you are really my disciples. Then you will know the truth, and the truth will set you free.

2 Timothy 2:15

Do your best to present yourself to God as one approved, a workman who does not need to be ashamed and who correctly handles the word of truth.

2 Timothy 3:16

All Scripture is inspired by God and is useful to teach us what is true and to make us realize what is wrong in our lives. It corrects us when we are wrong and teaches us to do what is right.

Psalm 109:19

Let it be to him as a garment with which he covers himself,
And for a belt with which he constantly girds himself.

1 John 1:18

If we say we have no sin, we deceive ourselves, and the truth is not in us.

Prayer:

Lord Jesus, have mercy on me. Please help me to know the truth, show me the truth, so I can understand your will and your ways. Open my spiritual eyes so that I will confess the truth with my mouth. Please help me to always tell the truth even when I don't want to so that I can be trustworthy and full of honor. Thank you for being here for me and for your patience with me and loving me even when I don't deserve it. Guide me in your truth and teach me your ways, for you are my God, my Savior and my hope is in you all day long.

In Jesus' mighty name, Amen.

Breastplate of Righteousness

Ephesians 6:14
Stand firm then, with the breastplate of righteousness in place.

What is the Breastplate of Righteousness?
Who is Righteous?

We must wear the breastplate to protect our heart. Our heart can be easily wounded and deceived if we aren't guarding it. Righteousness means to be right with God by choosing to do the right thing. Those who stand strong in faith and do good by doing God's will are made righteous through Jesus, for there are none righteous without him. Only God makes us righteous.

Psalms 119:137
Righteous are you, Oh Lord, and your laws are right.
The statutes you have laid down are righteous.
They are fully trustworthy.

1 John 3:7
Dear children, do not let anyone lead you astray. He who does what is right is righteous. He who does what is wrong is of the devil because the devil has been sinning from the beginning.

Life Application:
In all things, we should do the right thing even when we don't feel like it. We have to put ourselves in other people's shoes and ask ourselves if what we are doing is what we would want someone to do to us. The rewards are much greater than the punishment we will cause for ourselves later. Sometimes the rewards for doing the right thing may have to wait and that's okay, just remember that God is faithful to His promises and is always watching over us. He will reward us in His perfect time. He is always Righteous and worthy of our praise.

Matthew 5:6 & 10
Blessed are those who hunger and thirst for righteousness, for

they will be filled. Blessed are those who are persecuted because of righteousness, for theirs is the kingdom of heaven.

Matthew 13:49

This is how it will be at the end of the age. The angels will come and separate the wicked from the righteous and throw them into the fiery furnace.

Philippians 3:9

I no longer count on my own righteousness through obeying the law; rather, I become righteous through faith in Christ. For God's way of making us right with himself depends on faith.

Romans 5:19

Because one person disobeyed God, many became sinners. But because one other person obeyed God, many will be made righteous.

Romans 13:12

The night is almost gone, and the day is near. Therefore let us lay aside the deeds of darkness and put on the armor of light.

Psalm 18:24

So the Lord repaid me according to my righteousness; he repaid me according to the cleanness of my hands.

Prayer:

Lord Jesus, please forgive me of my sins. Cleanse me and transform my mind and heart. Fill me with Your Holy Spirit. Please help me to make the right choices and strengthen my heart and mind to do good things that are pleasing to you. Help me love others even when I don't feel like it so that I will be righteous in your sight. Help me to be faithfully and to serve you in all that I hear, think, see, say, and do. Thank you for guarding and protecting me when I need it. Thank you for walking with me through hard times and for choosing me to be your heir, your adopted child, whom you love.

In Jesus' mighty name, Amen.

Gospel Shoes of Peace

Ephesians 6:15
And with your feet fitted with the readiness
that comes from the gospel of peace.

What are the Gospel shoes?
Who can wear them?

Christians wear the Gospel Shoes of Peace to deliver God's message. We take the word of God by faith and share His word with others by spreading the good news of Jesus Christ to everyone, with thanksgiving and peace in our hearts! When we hear God's word, read God's word, study His word, memorize His word and pray. It helps us to know Him richly and gives us the spiritual food needed to share Him with confidence.

The Great commandment ~ Matthew 22:37
"Love the Lord your God with all your heart, and with all your soul and with all your mind. This is the first and greatest commandment. The second is like it: Love your neighbor as yourself.

The Great Commission ~ Matthew 28:19-20
Go and make disciples of all nations, baptizing them in the name of the Father, Son, and Holy Spirit and teaching them to obey everything I have commanded you. Surely, I am with you always, till the very end of the age.

Life Application:

We should share the love of Jesus with our family and friends or anyone else that God puts in our lives and not be ashamed. Trusting Jesus to guide our footsteps is crucial so that we will not stumble or cause others to stumble and fall. Walk-in peace and in love. Encourage others to do the right thing too. Once Jesus comes into our lives, and fills our heart with his love, we should honor him by publicly being baptized by water just as Jesus did to celebrate our new life as believers and to show our commitment to

Him. It's important to be connected through God's word and to fellowship with other Christians. Try going to church and volunteering to help others. Take communion regularly. Always work hard and do your best and know that you are deeply loved.

Matthew 5:9

Blessed are the peacemakers, for they shall be called the sons of God.

Psalms 119:105

Your word is a lamp unto my feet and a light unto my path.

Galatians 5:22

But the Holy Spirit produces this kind of fruit in our lives: love, joy, peace, patience, kindness, goodness, faithfulness.

Philippians 4:4-6

Do not be anxious about anything, but in every situation, by prayer and petition, with thanksgiving, present your requests to God. And the peace of God, which surpasses all understanding will guard your heart and your mind in Christ Jesus.

Romans 14:19

So let's strive for the things that bring peace and the things that build each other up.

Numbers 6:26

May the Lord show you his favor and give you his peace.

Prayer:

Lord Jesus, give me the strength and courage to go out into the world and spread the good news. Let your words be a lamp unto my feet and a light unto my path. Teach me to speak and act more like You. Grant me the wisdom and understanding I need so that I can forgive anyone who hurts me. Please give me peace in my heart that only you can give and help me to do the best that I can. May Your light shine upon me and give me a new hope, filled with Your blessings, Your love and Your joy so that I can be a light to lead others to you.

In Jesus' mighty name, Amen!

Shield of Faith

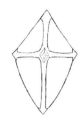

Ephesians 6:16
Take up the shield of faith with which you can
extinguish all the flaming arrows of the evil one.

What is the shield of faith?
Why do I need it?

Faith is something we hope for but can not see. Faith is believing that God exists even though we can't see Him in person.
The shield of faith protects us from Satan and his army. If we need more faith, we can ask Jesus for it. Satan will try to get us to do the wrong things. If we aren't careful, we will easily find ourselves going down the wrong path leading to sin. We cannot stand against Satan on our own; he is too powerful. Only by the power and blood of Jesus can we overcome the evil ones.

2 Samuel 22:31-32

As for God, his way is perfect; the word of the Lord is flawless. He is a shield for all to take refuge in him. For who is God besides the Lord? And who is the rock except for our God?

1 John 5:4

For everyone born of God overcomes the world. This is the victory that has overcome the world, even our faith. Who is it that overcomes the world? Only he who believes that Jesus is the son of God.

Life Application:

Faith is a gift; if we want more of it, we need to pray and ask Jesus to grant it to us so that our faith will grow stronger. We must have faith that God will protect us and provide for all of our needs. We often have to take a step of faith first to see God move in our lives. Remember He's not a genie in the bottle and may not answer all our prayers the way we want Him to and that's ok.

Matthew 7:7

Jesus says, "Ask, and it will be given, seek, and you shall find, knock, and the door will be opened."

Hebrews 11:1

Now faith is the substance of things hoped for, the evidence of things not seen.

Matthew 17:20

If you have faith as small as a mustard seed, you can say to this mountain, move from here to there, and it will move. Nothing will be impossible for you.

Mark 4:30

The kingdom of God is described as a mustard seed, which is the smallest seed you plant in the ground. Yet when planted, it grows and becomes the largest of all garden plants, with such big branches that birds can perch in its shade.

Hebrew 11:6

And without faith it is impossible to please God, because anyone who comes to him must believe that he exists and that he rewards those who earnestly seek him.

1 Corinthians 16:13-14

Be on your guard, stand firm in the faith, be people of courage, be strong. Do everything in love.

Philippians 4:13

I can do All things through Christ who strengthens me.

Prayer:

Heavenly Father, you are my shield, my armor, my all in all. Thank you for sending your son Jesus to die on the cross for me and for allowing me to come before you to make my requests known. I ask that you strengthen my faith, bless my family and friends and protect us from harm's way. Send your guardian angels to guide my footsteps down the path that I am to go. Thank you for giving me more faith and courage. Thank you for forgiving me of all my sins from the past, present and future. Thank you for your faithfulness and ever lasting love.

In Jesus' mighty name, Amen.

Helmet of Salvation

Ephesians 6:17
Take up the helmet of salvation and the sword
of the spirit, which is the word of God.

**What is salvation? Where does it come from?
How do I get it?**

Salvation is a free gift of eternal life, and salvation comes directly
from God alone. God sent his only son to die for us so that we can
have eternal life with Him. It is by grace; we are saved. We can't
earn it. We get it by believing and trusting in God's mighty word.
The only time God gives us permission to question Him is when
we are discovering who He is. Ask Him to reveal Himself to you if
you don't already know Him. Find a Bible or a person of true faith
and dig into His word to search out the truth.

John 3:16
For God so loved the world that he gave his only begotten son so
that whosoever believes in him should not perish but have eternal
life.

Acts 4:12
Neither is there salvation in any other: for there is no other name
under heaven given unto men by which we must be saved.

Life Application:
In order to enter heaven, we must truly believe that God is who
He says He is. He is the creator of the heavens and the earth. He is
the Alpha and Omega, the Beginning and the End. His words are
the same yesterday, today, and forever. By believing and trusting in
God, we carry faith in our hearts, praising Jesus as our Lord and
Savior. Jesus freed us from our debt of sin. We must guard our
hearts, minds, and thoughts against any wrong thinking that will
cause us to keep sinning. When we turn away from sin, we
become blameless.

Psalms 62:1
My soul finds rest in God alone; my salvation comes from him.

He alone is my rock and my salvation. He is my fortress. I will never be shaken.

Isaiah 59:17
He put on righteousness as his breastplate and the helmet of salvation on his head; he put on the garments of vengeance and wrapped himself in zeal as in a cloak.

Romans: 12:2
Do not conform any longer to the patterns of this world, but be transformed by the renewing of your mind. Then you will be able to attest and approve what God's will is, his good, pleasing, and perfect will.

1 Peter 1:13-15
Prepare your mind for action and exercise self control. Put all your hope in the gracious salvation that will come to you when Jesus Christ is revealed to the world. So you must live as Christ's obedient children. Don't slip back to your old ways of living to satisfy your own desire. You didn't know any better then…

1John 4:4
You are of God, little children, and have overcome them: because greater is he that is in you than he that is in the world.

Romans 10:9
If you declare with your mouth, "Jesus is Lord," and believe in your heart that God raised him from the dead, you'll be saved.

Prayer:
Lord Jesus, I know that I am a sinner. Please forgive me for all of my sins and give me a clear understanding of how I can honor you. Please help me to know the plans that you have for me and help me to be a good example for others to follow. Fill me with the power of your love, grace, and forgiveness so that I can be a light in the world to encourage others to follow you, to do good and not evil. Thank you for being my savior, my salvation, and my all in all. Thank you for adopting me into your family and for granting me the gift of eternal life to be with you in heaven, forever.

In Jesus' mighty name, Amen.

Sword of the Spirit

Ephesians 6:18
Pray in the spirit on all occasions with all kinds
of prayers and requests. Be alert and always
keep praying.

What is the sword of the spirit? How does it work?

The Sword of the Spirit is God's word. We must learn to use God's word correctly and protect it with all our hearts. We have to guard our words so that they do not hurt others. Instead, let's use our words to build each other up and encourage those around us who need comforted. We can speak good or bad things with the power of our tongues. God wants us to know Him personally, and He wants us to know ourselves as well as He knows us! We can know in our hearts that the spirit of God lives in us by what we say and do. We must learn to plant His word in our mind and our heart so when the time calls for it, we can defend God's mighty word.

Romans 8:14
Those who are led by the spirit of God are sons of God. For you did not receive a spirit that makes you a slave again to fear, but you received the spirit of sonship. And by him, we cry Abba Father. The spirit himself testifies with our spirit that we are God's children.

2 Corinthians 10:3-4
For though we live in the world, we do not wage war as the world does. The weapons we fight with are not the weapons of the world. On the contrary, they have divine power to demolish strongholds.

Life Application:
Our lives are like the seeds that are planted in this world. The seeds we produce can be good or bad. If properly cared for, then we will produce good fruits, and our seeds will prosper, but if we aren't careful with our words and actions, then our seeds won't

produce good fruit but will wither and die. Let's be productive and produce good fruit that pleases God. Let's stay connected to Jesus by talking to Him everyday through prayer. It's important to have fellowship with other believers who strengthen us. Reading the Bible daily will strengthen our heart and mind. Our words are like a two-edged sword! Iron sharpens iron, so must we learn to sharpen iron by what we say and do.

Matthew 10:32-34
Whosoever acknowledges me before men, I will also acknowledge him before my Father in heaven, but whoever disowns me before men, I will disown him before my Father in heaven. Do not suppose that I have come to bring peace to the earth, but a sword.

Acts 2:4
All of them were filled with the Holy Spirit and began to speak in other tongues as the Spirit enabled them.

Acts 4:31
After they prayed, the place where they were meeting was shaken. And they were all filled with the Holy Spirit and spoke the word of God boldly.

John 1:1
In the beginning was the word, and the word was with God, and the word was God.

Prayer:

Lord Jesus, thank you for all that you've done, for all that you are doing, and for what is yet to come. Please help me to control my tongue so that I will not sin against you by the things I say. Protect my mind, body, and soul against my enemies who wish me harm. Please give me the wisdom to speak the truth with confidence and boldness. Guard my thoughts against wanting to do the wrong things. Plant your seeds of love, hope, and faith in my heart so that they will prosper and grow, giving me the ability to share with others what you have freely given to me. I pray for your favor to be on my life and those around me.

In Jesus' mighty name, Amen.

A GLOBAL QUEST

Kem Arfaras

Armor of God
Ephesians 6:13-19
New English Translation

13 For this reason, take up the full armor of God so that you may be able to stand your ground on the evil day, and having done everything, to stand. **14** Stand firm therefore, by fastening the belt of truth around your waist, by putting on the breastplate of righteousness, **15** by fitting your feet with the preparation that comes from the good news of peace, **16** and in all of this, by taking up the shield of faith with which you can extinguish all the flaming arrows of the evil one. **17** And take *the helmet of salvation* and the sword of the Spirit (which is the word of God). **18** With every prayer and petition, pray at all times in the Spirit, and to this end be alert, with all perseverance and petitions for all the saints. **19** Pray for me also, that I may be given the right words.

Is your name written in the Lamb's Book of Life?

Join the quest and sign up today!

TELL ME WHAT YOU LIKED MOST AND LEAST!

adventureswithathens1@gmail.com

Learn how to become a warrior for Jesus and an heir to His everlasting kingdom!

This is where one story ends and a new adventure begins.

Help share the message of hope and love around the world by supporting this ministry. You will be helping to get this book and program into many hands and hearts of young people worldwide.

God Bless you as you partner with us to make a noble global impact. We can change lives one step at a time!

FOR MORE INFORMATION, PLEASE CONTACT ME BY EMAIL:

adventureswithathens1@gmail.com

Soon to come will be a complete guide with detailed information to go along with a new program for putting on the full Armor of God. It will be exciting to see lives being transformed by the anointing power of God!

My God Who Is HE ....

El Shaddai - (God Almighty), Elohim - (One True God), Emmanuel (God with us), El Elyon - (Most High God), Extraordinary, Exact, Exceptional, Essential, Ethical, Eternal, Exemplified, Exalted, Equipped, Elevated, Enlightened, Esteemed, Enriched, Engaged, Enraged, Elated, Ecstatic, Empathetic, Exotic, Enthusiastic, Exhorter, Energizer, Encourager, Excellent, Expert, Eminent, Exuberant, Eloquent, Efficient, Earnest, Everlasting, Edifying, Empowering, Exhilarating, Endearing, Entertaining, Enduring, Elaborate, Exquisite, Effective, Enjoyable, Endless. He is my Everything and will never be Extinct!   By: Kem Arfaras

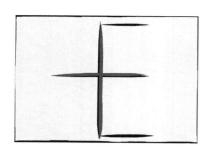

USA ~ THAILAND

USA ~ INDIA

USA ~ ISRAEL ~ VBS

LOCAL & GLOBAL
MISSIONS

Tarpon Springs Florida

Hebrews 12:1-3

New Living Translation

God's Discipline Proves His Love
Therefore, since we are surrounded by such a huge crowd of witnesses to the life of faith, let us strip off every weight that slows us down, especially the sin that so easily trips us up. And let us run with endurance the race God has set before us. We do this by keeping our eyes on Jesus, the champion who initiates and perfects our faith. Because of the joy awaiting Him, He endured the cross, disregarding its shame. Now He is seated in the place of honor beside God's throne. Think of all that he endured from sinful people; then you won't become weary and give up.

The World

ABOUT THE AUTHOR

Kem's love for literary expression took root as an honored elementary school student whose poems were showcased in its periodical. She wrote her first short story at the age of ten and holds the only copy. Her heart strings are children. By the age of six Kem's world had been turned upside down. Her biological father had abandoned the family; her mother was nearly killed in a car crash and she was separated from her siblings for a time. But then there was God who saw her and transformed her life. Kem is a wife, mother, aunt, sister and grandmother. She also loves photography, and teaching the Word of God through scripture and personal life experiences. She's a missionary at heart and has traveled the globe making friends around the world. Kem has three children, four grandchildren, and a marriage of 35 years to a first-generation Greek American.

In the midst of it all, her insatiable love for children still hadn't been pacified, so she opened a daycare and a preschool for many years while raising her own family in Florida. She taught Pre-K and Art from Pre-K through High School at Tampa Christian Community School while pursuing her life's crown jewel. She has spent much of her life ministering and volunteering in various places worldwide to help further the Kingdom of God. She's been chosen several times to take part in helping to lead many Bible schools globally, teaching the true anointing power of God's Word. It's her life dream to build settings around the world for putting on the full Armor of God, helping people of all ages come to know the true anointing power of God, while leading as many souls as possible to Jesus before leaving this great planet Earth.

Her literary style is intentionally magical, adventurous, and whimsical, leaving no rock unturned, it's sure to inspire and coerce the reader to embrace the timelessness that can only be found in an open book and in the open arms of one Godhead found in Jesus Christ. Her hope is to be as much of a blessing to you as He's been to her!

Journey-Wise

Romans 12:2

A & A Print Shop of Tampa Bay, Florida